"I Think We Should Get Married,"

Justin said. "You said you needed a husband to get custody of your late sister's children. I'm the one you need."

Amy's stomach took a dip at his words. "But we don't love each other."

"Exactly," he agreed.

"We don't really even like each other."

"I don't agree with that," he said. "I like you."

"Why would you do this?"

Justin paused a moment. "This is hard to explain. You know how you have this strong feeling that part of your purpose in life is to help those disadvantaged preschoolers?"

Amy nodded, but the connection eluded her.

"I *know* I'm supposed to marry you," Justin concluded. "*You* are one of my reasons for being on this planet."

MILLION DOLLAR MEN

These wealthy bachelors form a club
to make others' dreams come true...
and find the women of *their* dreams in return!

Dear Reader,

Welcome to the world of Silhouette Desire, where you can indulge yourself every month with romances that can only be described as passionate, powerful and provocative!

The incomparable Diana Palmer heads the Desire lineup for March. *The Winter Soldier* is a continuation of the author's popular cross-line miniseries, SOLDIERS OF FORTUNE. We're sure you'll enjoy this tale of a jaded hero who offers protection in the form of a marriage of convenience to a beautiful woman in jeopardy.

Bestselling author Leanne Banks offers you March's MAN OF THE MONTH, a tempting *Millionaire Husband,* book two of her seductive miniseries MILLION DOLLAR MEN. The exciting Desire continuity series TEXAS CATTLEMAN'S CLUB: LONE STAR JEWELS continues with *Lone Star Knight* by Cindy Gerard, in which a lady of royal lineage finds love with a rugged Texas cattle baron.

The M.D. Courts His Nurse as Meagan McKinney's miniseries MATCHED IN MONTANA returns to Desire. And a single-dad rancher falls for the sexy horsetrainer he unexpectly hires in Kathie DeNosky's *The Rough and Ready Rancher*. To cap off the month, Shawna Delacorte writes a torrid tale of being *Stormbound with a Tycoon.*

So make some special time for yourself this month, and read all six of these tantalizing Silhouette Desires!

Enjoy!

Joan Marlow Golan

Joan Marlow Golan
Senior Editor, Silhouette Desire

Please address questions and book requests to:
Silhouette Reader Service
U.S.: 3010 Walden Ave., P.O. Box 1325, Buffalo, NY 14269
Canadian: P.O. Box 609, Fort Erie, Ont. L2A 5X3

Millionaire Husband
LEANNE BANKS

Silhouette®

Desire

Published by Silhouette Books

America's Publisher of Contemporary Romance

SILHOUETTE BOOKS

ISBN 0-373-76352-2

MILLIONAIRE HUSBAND

Copyright © 2001 by Leanne Banks

All rights reserved. Except for use in any review, the reproduction or utilization of this work in whole or in part in any form by any electronic, mechanical or other means, now known or hereafter invented, including xerography, photocopying and recording, or in any information storage or retrieval system, is forbidden without the written permission of the editorial office, Silhouette Books, 300 East 42nd Street, New York, NY 10017 U.S.A.

All characters in this book have no existence outside the imagination of the author and have no relation whatsoever to anyone bearing the same name or names. They are not even distantly inspired by any individual known or unknown to the author, and all incidents are pure invention.

This edition published by arrangement with Harlequin Books S.A.

® and TM are trademarks of Harlequin Books S.A., used under license. Trademarks indicated with ® are registered in the United States Patent and Trademark Office, the Canadian Trade Marks Office and in other countries.

Visit Silhouette at www.eHarlequin.com

Printed in U.S.A.

Books by Leanne Banks

LEANNE BANKS

is a national number-one bestselling author of romance. She lives in her native Virginia with her husband, son and daughter. Recognized for both her sensual and humorous writing with two Career Achievement Awards from *Romantic Times Magazine,* Leanne likes creating a story with a few grins, a generous kick of sensuality and characters who hang around after the book is finished. Leanne believes romance readers are the best readers in the world because they understand that love is the greatest miracle of all. You can write to her at P.O. Box 1442, Midlothian, VA 23113. An SASE for a reply would be greatly appreciated.

This book is dedicated to the stock jock
with *cojones,* brains and heart.

Thank you for everything!

One

Another day, another hundred thousand dollars. With the exception of the nagging pain in his abdomen, Justin Langdon was feeling pretty pleased as he climbed the steps to Edward St. Albans Elementary school. The *St. Albans Chronicle* didn't call him their top stock jock for nothing. Popping two antacids, he thought the beautiful thing about the stock market was that a shrewd man could make money when it went up and when it went down. Justin believed in doing both.

After a childhood spent at the Granger Home for Boys, Justin had worked a day job and put every penny he had on making money in the stock market.

His tightwad days of eating beanee weenees had paid off, and he was now a multimillionaire. He was damn sure he wouldn't be eating cans of beans anymore. If his financial success occasionally rang hollow, he didn't dwell on it. Besides, two of his highly successful alumni buddies from the Granger Home for Boys had talked him into joining them in a secret, tax deductible, charitable foundation, the Millionaires' Club.

Justin still had moments of doubt over his commitment to the Millionaires' Club, but he would do his duty. He walked through the hallway of the aging elementary school toward the sounds of young children. Justin's charity assignment was to investigate the after-school program to determine whether the Millionaires' Club should donate and how much.

Absently rubbing his stomach, he rounded the hall corner and peered into the noisy classroom. A curvy woman with a mop of red curly hair and dressed as a *J* led the youngsters in a song of words starting with the letter *J*. Was this Amy Monroe, the director of the program? Her feminine curves and one hundred and fifty watt smile nearly distracted him from the fact that the red costume clashed with her hair. She gestured and danced for the children, encouraging them when their volume grew. He'd never seen so much enthusiasm inside one single person before.

"Jack, jam, Japan, jar!"

Justin's stomach clenched and he frowned. It must be the noise, he thought, but he couldn't deny Miss Monroe's effectiveness. He was almost tempted to join in the chorus too.

Amy spied him and waved at him. "Come in and join us," she called, then smiled at the children. "Join starts with—?"

"*J!*" they chorused.

Justin moved into the room and slid into a too-small chair. His stomach seemed to nag him more than usual, but he pushed the pain aside, telling himself it was the result of overexposure to so many noisy children at once.

Justin didn't hate kids. From his upbringing, however, he'd learned that a wife, ex-wife and children constituted the biggest sucking sound a man could possibly experience in his bank account. That lesson had been driven home to him month after month when his divorced mother received the child support payment from his dad and subsequently shopped till she dropped. She and Justin always ended up with more month than money left, eventually necessitating his move to the Granger Home for Boys. Justin had vowed never to put himself or anyone else he cared for in that position again in his life. That meant no marriage and no kids.

Amy Monroe's curves distracted him again. His no-marriage rule didn't mean no dating, he told himself, remembering his good friend Michael's advice for him to drag himself away from the computer and get out more.

"See you Thursday," she said, dismissing the class. "We're doing *K* then."

Justin stood as the kids stampeded past him. A hush immediately descended on the room, and he met Amy's gaze. "You're Amy Monroe, the pre-school special-program coordinator," he said.

She nodded. "And you're Justin Langdon. I received a message that you might be coming to observe, but no explanation." She gave him a curious glance. "Do you have a child you want to enter into the program?"

"Oh, no. I'm doing some research on your program. You looked like you were getting through to them," he said. "I'd like to hear more about it. Can I take you to dinner tonight?"

Amy Monroe felt a sliver of temptation and ignored it. She also ignored the fact that Justin Langdon's intelligent gaze perked her interest. She ignored his chiseled bone structure and the curve of his lips that hinted at sensuality. She told herself not to think about how his broad shoulders promised strength and protection. She ignored the hum of electric awareness shooting between them. She ignored all these things because she had to ignore them. Although Amy couldn't remember the last time she'd joined a handsome intelligent man for dinner, she knew she had no room in her life for dates. She shook her head. "I'm sorry. Tonight's bad."

He shrugged. "Tomorrow night then?"

"Tomorrow's bad, too. Actually every night for the next year is probably going to be bad."

He blinked. "Why?"

"Three reasons," she said and decided to kill all the interest at once. "Their ages are five, three and three. My kids," she said, because since her sister and brother-in-law had died eight weeks ago, Emily, Jeremy and Nick had become her kids.

Justin Langdon blinked again. If she didn't know better, she'd swear he even turned pale with disbelief. "You have three children," he said. "I didn't see a ring—"

"Oh, I'm not married. I've never been married."

"I can see why you'd be busy, then." Justin rubbed his stomach absently. "Is there a restroom?"

"Sure, right through that door," Amy said, pointing to the rear of the room. She grew concerned at the odd expression on his face. "Are you okay?"

He made a vague sound and headed for the restroom.

Amy frowned. She realized children frightened many men, but she hadn't expected his look of near-nausea. Shrugging, she quickly put the classroom in order so she could leave. Hearing a strangled cough, she felt a tinge of uneasiness. "Mr. Langdon," she called, knocking on the door. "Justin, are you all right?"

He coughed again.

Her uneasiness growing by the second, she knocked again. "Mr. Langdon, are you decent?"

"Yes, but—"

Amy pushed open the door and saw that the man's handsome face had turned ashen. He held a paper towel in his hand stained with bright red blood. "Nose bleed?"

He shook his head. "I coughed."

Alarm tightened her chest. She didn't know what the blood meant, but she knew it wasn't good. "You need to get to the hospital."

Justin protested the pushy woman for about forty-five seconds until he felt the urge to cough again. Then he focused his energy on not coughing and fighting the light-headed feeling that settled over him like a thick fog. In the occasional moments the fog lifted, Justin noticed Amy Monroe drove her Volkswagen Beetle like a bat out of hell and swore in a very un-teacher-like fashion at drivers who moved too slowly to suit her.

Pain burned through his gut, stealing his breath and sense of humor. He felt her quick glance of concern.

"Breathe," she told him.

"In a minute," he muttered, hating the combination of pain and fuzziness.

"No," she said. "Breathe. You're tensing up. That makes the pain worse. It's like childbirth. If you breathe, you can stay on top of it."

"You should know," Justin said and drew in a ragged breath. Lethargy dragged at him. He felt as if someone was pressing two hundred pound weights on his eyelids. If he could just rest for a few minutes...

"Mr. Langdon! Justin!"

Wincing at the pain, he didn't open his eyes. "What?"

"We're almost at the hospital."

He'd never felt so tired. It occurred to Justin that he should thank her for bringing him. He struggled to open his mouth, but couldn't. Frustration swirled inside him.

The car jerked to a stop and he felt a flurry of activity. He heard voices.

"—coughing up blood," Amy Monroe said. "I think his stomach is hurting."

"...ulcer. He may need surgery," a male voice said.

Justin tried to protest, but again he couldn't. He focused all his energy on opening his eyes and found himself staring into Amy Monroe's worried gaze. He opened his mouth. "Thank—"

She put her finger over his lips and shook her

head. "Save your strength. We were all put on this earth for a reason. You're one of my reasons today. Breathe," she said and brushed her soft mouth against his cheek.

Justin felt himself wheeled over the pavement through the doors. The pain mounting, he stopped fighting and allowed his eyes to close. The hospital faded away and his world turned dark.

"Emergency surgery," he heard a woman say, and then he heard no more.

A vision wafted through his mind. His good friends Michael and Dylan shook their heads. "So young," Michael said.

"What a waste," Dylan said. "All he did was work and worry about money."

Michael's wife Kate took his hand. "He never really got it," she said sadly. "I think he was right on the edge, but he never really got it."

Got what? Justin wondered.

"He fought it," Dylan said.

Fought what? Justin wanted to know.

Michael nodded. "I can't believe he didn't have a will. He would turn over if he knew how much the government was getting of his fortune."

Will! Panic sliced through him. He'd never made a will because he'd always assumed he had time. He broke into a cold sweat. Was he dead?

Kate wiped a tear from her eye. "I wish he could

have had more. It feels like such a waste. I can't imagine getting to the end of my life and knowing I could have made a difference, but didn't. I can't imagine never loving someone. It's such a waste," she said and Michael took her into his arms.

Justin wondered if he was dead. All the things he'd intended to do later raced through his head. Worst of all, however, was the incredibly empty feeling that engulfed him. His throat tightened with dread. Had his life really been all for naught? He'd been so busy trading and adding to his wealth, adding to his financial security that he couldn't even see anything, let alone anyone else.

What had he done to make the world a better place?

The regret felt like a tidal wave, drowning him with a thousand should-haves.

If you're out there, God, I'm sorry. I've screwed up big time. If you can give me a second chance...

Ridiculous notion, Justin thought. If Justin were God, why would he give Justin a second chance? What had Justin done to deserve another chance?

Well, hell, Justin thought. Maybe God wasn't a self-centered jerk like Justin was. Maybe God was smarter and better than he was. Maybe God was nicer. Maybe God believed in second chances.

If you can give me a second chance, I'll try to figure out the real reason you put me on this earth and get it done.

* * *

Justin wished whoever was putting fifty-pound bags of cement on his eyelids would stop. He frowned, concentrating with the effort to open his eyes.

"Looks like he's waking up," a familiar voice said. Through the fog of his mind, he tried to place the voice.

"Hey, Justin, welcome back to the land of the living," another familiar voice said.

Justin blinked and looked into the faces of his two friends, Michael Hawkins and Dylan Barrows.

"You gave everyone a scare," Michael said, his observant gaze crinkled with concern. It occurred to Justin that Michael seemed more human since he'd married and become a father.

"I know you've been dragging your feet on this after-school reading program donation," Dylan said, "but was surgery really preferable?"

Justin felt a grin grow inside him. He gave a rough chuckle. Pain sliced through his side. He swore under his breath. "Show some mercy, Dylan."

Dylan shook his head. "You look like a truck ran over you."

"Thank you," Justin said wryly.

"No, really," Dylan said, his face growing serious. He gave Justin's arm a quick squeeze. "You need to take better care of yourself. I don't want anything bad to happen to you. Even if you are a cheapskate, you're a good guy.''

A fleeting image of his Scrooge-like dream oozed through his mind and his humor faded. ''Maybe not good enough,'' he muttered to himself.

''I hate to run, but I booked this charter last week,'' Dylan said regretfully. ''I'll rest easy knowing you're okay.''

''Charter to Rio or Paris?'' Justin asked, mildly curious. Dylan was always running here or there. At times, it almost seemed as if Dylan was running from himself.

''Neither. The Caribbean. Weekend in Belize. Maybe you can go with me when you're feeling better.''

''Blonde or brunette?'' Justin asked.

Dylan cracked a grin that didn't extend to his eyes and waved his hand. ''Neither this time. I invited Alisa Jennings, but she turned me down flat. Third time this month.''

''For someone with a healthy ego, you seem to have none where she is concerned.''

''Glutton for punishment, I guess. I'll just do a little fishing and diving and a lot of thinking.'' He glanced at his gold watch, then back at Justin. ''Take care, bud. I'll see you when I get back. You too, Michael.''

As soon as Dylan left, Justin met Michael's gaze. ''Dylan? Thinking?''

"He's pretty hooked on Alisa."

"I'm surprised he didn't just go on to the next one. Dylan always seems like he's got a string of women waiting for him."

"I think he and Alisa were more involved than he admits."

"That's what I always thought," Justin said, fighting a sudden weariness.

"But enough about Dylan. You look like you're ready to drift off again, so I'll leave—"

"Just a minute," Justin said. "I, uh…I guess I could have croaked."

"Yeah," Michael said with a nod.

His chest tightened and he brushed the sensation aside. "I thought about everything I hadn't done."

"Like going to Belize?" Michael asked with a grin.

Justin shook his head. "No. Important stuff." Strange emotions tugged at him and he shrugged. "You seem like you're at peace. Why?"

"Oh, that's easy. Kate and the baby. When it's all said and done, everyone and everything else might leave, but I know I'll still have Kate." He paused. "And I like what I'm doing with you and Dylan. It's fun and more." He chuckled to himself. "Kate says the three of us suffer from a fraud complex about our wealth. I guess giving some of it away makes me feel less like a fraud." Michael studied him. "You need to rest," he said. "You'll be okay."

Distantly aware of Michael leaving his room, Justin struggled with the haze settling over him. He thought about what Michael had said and shook his head. He couldn't believe his purpose had anything to do with being a husband and father. Closing his eyes, Justin decided he would just have to keep looking.

Three weeks later, Justin still had a gnawing sensation inside him but, thank goodness, it had nothing to do with an ulcer. Needing to thank Amy Monroe for getting him to the hospital, he found her address and drove to her house after the stock market closed. He pulled into the driveway behind Amy's Volkswagen. He scanned the area and noted the large older two-story home in a neighborhood filled with oaks, weeping willow trees and kids, at least a dozen kids.

Snatching the bouquet of roses from the passenger seat and getting out of his car, he climbed the small, slightly tilted porch and rang the doorbell. A little girl with lopsided pigtails quickly appeared and stared him up and down. "A man is at the door," she yelled at the top of her lungs.

Just then, two toddler boys raced to the door and stared at him. One poked his thumb in his mouth.

Twins, Justin noted, thankful again that fatherhood was not part of his purpose.

Amy appeared, dressed in shorts that emphasized her long shapely legs. Affectionately ruffling the hair of one of the twins, she glanced at the flowers and Justin in surprise. Her gaze searched his and she smiled.

Justin's heart gave an odd, unexpected jump.

Amy opened the door. "Come in. I called the hospital a few times to make sure you survived my driving. How are you? Was it an ulcer?"

"I'm much better," he said and nodded. "Yes, it was an ulcer. After surgery, the treatment was antibiotics." He had felt sheepish when he'd learned his emergency could have been prevented with a simple prescription.

"Guys hate going to the doctor, don't they?" she mused.

"This one does," he said and extended the bouquet of roses. "These are for you. Thank you for saving my life." Flowers weren't nearly enough, but Justin wasn't stopping there. He had other plans for Amy and her after-school program.

"You're welcome," she said, taking the roses in her arms. The two tykes wrapped their arms around each of her legs.

Justin couldn't blame the little guys for wanting to be close to her. She radiated a combination of optimism, feminine strength and nurturing that would draw boys, both little and big, and she wore her undeniable sensuality like a spellbinding exotic perfume.

She glanced down at the boys. "Oops. I've forgotten my manners. Justin Langdon, allow me to introduce my kids, Jeremy, Nick and Emily. Smell the beautiful roses," she said dipping the bouquet to pint-size level, then she turned to Emily. "Would you mind getting me a vase with water, sweetheart? There's one under the sink. Dinner's almost ready, so everyone needs to wash up."

Faster than a speeding bullet, the twins detached themselves and tore out of the room.

"Me first!" Nick said.

"*Me* first!" Jeremy said.

"Chicken and dumplings is one of their favorite dinners," Amy explained. "Comfort food. We're very big on comfort food since my sister and her husband died."

Justin frowned. "Your sister died recently?"

Amy nodded, sadness muting the lively glint in her brown eyes. "And her husband. The children lost mom and dad in one day."

Justin digested the new information. "They're not your children?"

"They're mine now," she said firmly. "And they're staying with me regardless of what any social worker says about my age or anything else."

Justin got the uncomfortable impression that there was a story here, a story he'd just as soon not hear.

Emily reappeared and tugged on the hem of Amy's shirt. Amy bent down while the little girl whispered to her. Amy's smile emanated amusement and a hint of challenge. "Emily wants to know if you'd like to join us for dinner. The food should be safe, but our dinner table, uh, culture, may test your ulcer medication."

Justin glanced at two pairs of brown eyes and was surprised at his visceral response to both. Emily's gaze held a tinge of sadness that tugged at him. He couldn't help remembering long-buried feelings of abandonment from his own childhood, and the knowing provocative dare in Amy's eyes affected him in a wholly different way. He could learn about the after-school program, he told himself, justifying his immediate decision.

"I'd love to stay," he said, getting a sly sense of satisfaction from Amy's double take.

"You're sure?" she said, and he had the odd sense she was really saying *Are you man enough for this?*

Justin felt the click inside him. It was a quality he kept hidden from most people, a deadly serious determination to meet a goal, to prove himself. He'd experienced the sensation only a few times in his life and learned it was like flicking a lighter in a room filled with gasoline. It was what had won him a scholarship to college and what had kept him going during his years of eating cans of beanee weenees before he'd made his first million.

Something about Amy Monroe brought the same flame to life. She was a woman with sunshine in her eyes, a body with dangerous curves and even more dangerous dependents—children. He didn't know why, but he had the inexplicable urge to show Amy he was man enough for anything she might need.

Two

"I'd like to expand the program to at least five more elementary schools in this district," Amy said, responding to Justin's question about her after-school program at the same moment she saved Jeremy's cup from a spill. "I'd really like to make it county-wide, and if you want to know what I wish before I blow out the candles on my birthday cake, I'd love to see this spread all over the state, then the whole country." She paused, studying Justin's face. She knew some people felt overwhelmed by her dreams, but she sensed he understood at the same time he was amused.

"Amy, the Empress of Literacy," he said.

He made it sound more sexy than mocking, but perhaps that was just because *he* was sexy.

"I can't deny it," she said. "Two and a half hours per week could make a huge difference in the lives of the children who participate in the program."

"What do you need to make it happen? Money?"

"That would help," she said. "Teachers interested in helping with the program would find it more inviting to know their time and experience would be rewarded. The program also needs more exposure. It would be great if we became the darling of a women's organization, or a corporate sponsor decided to take us on, but since I became a mom," she said, smiling at Nick, Emily, and Jeremy, "I've had three of the best distractions in the world living with me." She noticed Nick squirming in his seat. "Bathroom?"

The little boy nodded. "I don't wanna miss dessert."

"Scoot. I promise to save some for you." After Nick left, she met Justin's inquiring gaze. "He waits a little too late sometimes," she explained. "Are you allowed to eat chocolate?"

His lips twitched, and his eyes flickered with a dangerous sensuality. "I'm allowed to eat anything I want," he said in a low voice that made her wonder what it would be like to be the subject of his undivided attention.

Distressed at her thoughts, Amy bit her lip and banished a wayward provocative image from her mind. If this was how she reacted to being dateless for six months, how would she act after a year? She cleared her throat and stood. "Good, then you can have a piece of the candy bar cake Emily and I made this afternoon."

Nick skidded into the room. "I'm back."

"Did you wash your hands?"

The little boy paused too long.

Amy chuckled and patted his head. "Finish the job and use soap."

"Are you a teacher like Aunt Amy?" Emily asked Justin.

As curious as her niece, Amy glanced over her shoulder to watch his response.

He shook his head. "I trade stocks."

"Which brokerage?" Amy asked.

He gave a casual shrug. "I trade online."

She gave him a second glance. He didn't look like a gambler. "What do you do when the market goes down?"

"When the market goes down, I short stocks."

Amy frowned as she placed a slice of cake on a plate. "Short?"

"I'm not gonna be short," Nick interrupted. "I'm gonna be tall."

Justin chuckled. "This doesn't have anything to do with height. Shorting a stock technically means you borrow the stock at one price hoping to replace it at a lower price. You place your order at a hopefully high price, then get out when it goes down. It's called shorting a stock.''

"I've never heard of it.''

"Only in America can you make or lose money on something you don't technically own. It's not for the faint of heart,'' Justin wryly said.

"Oh, makes for ulcers?'' she asked.

He paused. "Partly,'' he grudgingly admitted. "But not making money at all would make more ulcers.''

"What's an ulcer?'' Emily asked.

"It's something in your tummy that makes it hurt,'' Amy said.

"When my tummy hurts, I throw up,'' Jeremy said, then eyed the cake and quickly added, "but my tummy doesn't hurt now. My tummy is smiling because it's going to get cake.''

"My tummy is smiling bigger,'' Nick said.

"Is not,'' Jeremy said.

"Is too,'' Nick said.

"Is—''

"If your tummies don't shut up, you might not get cake,'' Emily pointed out.

Complete silence followed. For sixty seconds.

The doorbell rang.

"Is not,'' Jeremy whispered.

"I'll get it," Emily said, bounding from the kitchen.

Amy frowned as she set plates of cake in front of each twin. "Who could that—"

"It's Ms. Hatcher," Amy yelled from the foyer.

Amy's stomach sank.

She felt Justin's curious gaze on her. "Hatcher?"

"One of the social workers," she whispered. "I don't think she likes me."

He stood. "Why do you need a social worker? You're the closest living relative, aren't you?"

Amy nodded. "Yes, but my sister didn't have a will, so it's complicated." She glanced at the cake and winced. "She won't approve of the cake."

"Cake?" Justin echoed in disbelief. "What's wrong with cake?"

Amy shoved her hair from her face with the back of her arm. "She'll find something."

At the sound of heavy footsteps, Amy greeted the social worker with a bright smile. "Ms. Hatcher, what a surprise. We were just having dessert. Would you join us?"

The older woman gave a sharp glance to the boys and the messy chocolate cake. The boys' faces and hands were covered with chocolate. She sniffed in disapproval. "Sweets at this time of night will make it difficult for the children to sleep." She looked down her nose at Amy. "And it's unsafe for little Emily to answer the door. You should know better."

"I was cutting the—" Amy began and stopped. She didn't know why Ms. Hatcher so easily succeeded in making her feel inadequate. Amy had been trained to teach, and although she hadn't been trained to mother, she was determined to be the mother her niece and nephews desperately needed. "I'm sure you noticed that Emily may answer the door, but she doesn't open it unless she knows the visitor. Is there anything else I can help you with?"

"The health department will be making an inspection next week," Ms. Hatcher grudgingly reported.

Amy felt a trickle of relief. Progress, at last. "That's great news. That means we're one step closer."

"There are other steps in the process," Ms. Hatcher reminded her, glancing at Justin.

He extended his hand. "Justin Langdon. I met Amy through her after-school program. I'm sure you're familiar with the impressive results of her work."

Surprised at the alliance he offered, Amy met his green gaze and sent him a silent thank-you.

"I'm aware that Ms. Monroe has set a full plate for herself," Ms. Hatcher said. "You may see me to the door," she said to Amy.

Amy followed the woman to the foyer and endured Ms. Hatcher's lecture. After the social worker left, Amy leaned against the door. It was amazing how one person's presence could suck all the joy out of the air. Amy resented it. She didn't understand what Ms. Hatcher had against her. Although their first encounter hadn't been stellar, the woman couldn't seem to get past it. Amy knew the woman didn't approve of her. She disapproved of Amy's youth and the fact that she wasn't married. She seemed to disapprove of everything about Amy, yet the woman clearly didn't have valid grounds to prevent Amy from gaining custody of the children. The only thing Ms. Hatcher could do was make things difficult for Amy, and that was what the woman was doing.

Amy sighed and returned to the kitchen. The twins were licking their fingers and Emily had eaten the frosted perimeter and left the un-frosted center on her plate. All three faces were smudged with chocolate, all three content. Amy's heart twisted. Heaven help her, she loved these kids.

"We hated it," Justin said in a deadpan voice, lifting his empty plate and meeting Amy's gaze with a knowing look in his eyes. "You should have given us gruel instead."

"What's gruel?" Emily asked.

"Yucky, gross soup," Amy said, her lips twitching at Justin's joke. "Now you need to prove Ms. Hatcher wrong and get ready for bed."

All three groaned in unison.

"Why is that lady always so cranky?" asked Nick.

"She's mad at Aunt Amy because Aunt Amy slammed a baseball into her windshield and broke it," Emily said.

Amy felt Justin's intent gaze. Heat rose to her cheeks. "I apologized and paid for the repair," she felt compelled to say.

"She's still mad," Emily said, sadly shaking her pigtails.

"She needs to eat more cake," Jeremy suggested. "Can I have one more piece?"

"May I," Amy corrected. "And no, sweetie, you may not. First person ready for bed gets to pick the first bedtime story."

The three stampeded from the kitchen, leaving the room in abrupt silence.

Justin chuckled and shook his head. "You broke her windshield the first time you met her."

"It was an accident," she said, clearing the dishes from the table. "And it was technically before I met her." She shrugged. "How was I supposed to know she was going to pull into my driveway?"

"She reminds me of someone," Justin said.

"Named Atilla?" Amy asked, turning on the faucet to rinse the dishes.

"Close," he said. "I thought a house had already fallen on her."

Amy smiled at his reference to the witch in *The*

Wizard of Oz. "I'm sure that somewhere underneath her gruff exterior—"

"—lies a heart of stainless steel." His expression turned serious. "Can she prevent you from getting custody of the kids?"

Amy felt a ripple of unease. "I don't think so," she said. "She can just make things difficult. She doesn't approve of me."

"Any reason besides the baseball?"

"I'm too young, too employed, too single." Amy figured she would remain single for the rest of her life, and that was fine.

"And you smile too much," he said in that deadpan voice that made her smile at the same time her stomach danced. "You laugh too much. And her biggest objection is probably that you aren't ugly enough."

Not ugly enough. A forbidden pleasure rippled through her. "I'm not?"

He shook his head and stepped closer. "You need warts and an extra eye."

"You suppose she would like me then?"

"Maybe," he said. "You still might not be ugly enough even with warts and an extra eye."

She looked into his green eyes and wished she had a little more time and just a smidgeon more freedom. He was the most interesting man she'd met in a long time, and his mere presence in her house reminded her she was female. Amy heard Nick gargle. She had no time and no freedom, so she'd best just store up this moment for a rainy day.

"Thank you for coming tonight, Justin Langdon," she said and following a wayward impulse, she kissed him. Her mouth should have landed on his cheek. Instead, she pressed her lips against his surprised mouth. In two seconds, she caught a hint of his fire, his musky scent, and the taste of chocolate. The combination was seductive. She pulled back.

"Do you kiss every man whose life you save?" Justin asked.

Surprised at herself, Amy struggled for breath. "I don't save many lives. I used the Heimlich maneuver on a first grader when he tried to swallow an entire hot dog and he cried on me." She bit her lip. "Thank you for putting in a good word for me with Ms. Hatcher."

"Aunt Amy!" the twins chorused.

Regret and relief warred inside her. "I need to go. Can you let yourself out?"

He nodded, looking at her thoughtfully.

"G'night," she said. "And don't get your shorts in such a twist that you get another ulcer." She left him and the dishes, knowing the dishes would be there when she returned, but he would not.

Three stories, five songs, and lots of hugs later, Amy tucked first the boys, then Emily into bed, and softly closed the door. Sinking against the hallway wall, she crossed her arms over her chest and drank in the peace in the silence and darkness.

She struggled with the weariness that tried to settle on her shoulders. "I can do this," she whispered. "I can be what those children need me to be." Although Amy had always considered herself a fighter, strong enough for herself and anyone weaker, she was surprised at how tiring being a mom was. She was even more surprised by the loneliness.

Pushing away from the wall, she resolved to keep her weariness to herself. In time, it would fade. She hoped it would fade. Rounding the corner to the kitchen ready to face the dinner dishes, she stopped short at the sight that greeted her. She'd been right about one thing, wrong about the other. Justin Langdon was long gone. But he'd done the dishes.

Her heart twisted. She skimmed her fingers over the clean counter. Justin was an enigma. She found him extremely compelling. Another time, she might try to solve some of the mysteries she saw in his eyes. Amy thought of the kids and shook her head. In another life.

Justin climbed the steps to the front door of his town home in his well-lit, well-patrolled, quietly affluent neighborhood. He strode through the door and listened to the silence. After the noise and chaos of Amy's home, his house felt a little too quiet.

Justin scowled. That was impossible. Her home

symbolized everything he'd always wanted to avoid in his life. Dependents. He'd filled out countless tax forms answering "None" to the question "How many dependents?" Justin had always been determined to keep his answer at the nice safe, round number of zero. As a kid, he'd been disappointed so much by those who'd claimed him as a dependent that he never wanted to be in the position to disappoint.

He felt an odd uneasiness when he thought about Amy and her situation. She was taking on a lot of responsibility without much visible means of support. The memory of his promise to the Almighty wafted through his mind like a feather. Justin still knew he needed to find the reason he'd been put on this earth. Could it be related to Amy and the kids? His stomach clenched and he shook his head. That would involve the *D* word—dependents. Walking down the hardwood floors of the hall to his den which housed state-of-the-art video and stereo systems, Justin reached for an old James Bond DVD. With its Italian leather furniture and soft light, the room oozed comfort. He could easily imagine the sight of Amy lounging in his den, her lips inviting, her curves seductive. When she'd kissed him, he'd felt a ripple shoot to his groin. Her combination of power and sensuality alternately aroused his admiration and his baser instincts. He remembered she'd smelled like apple juice and sex.

A fleeting image of Amy's rugrats, cute though they may be, running wild in his peaceful domain made him twitch.

Justin shook off the images and slid the DVD into the player. He'd done her dishes and he would donate a tidy sum to her after-school program, but he was certain there was nothing else in the cards for him and Amy.

Over the next week, Justin pushed Amy from his mind and returned to his daily routine of trading on the stock market. At odd times during the day, however, her smiling face would sneak into his mind, her laughter would ring in his ears, and the remembered sensation of her lips against his would make his mouth buzz. Knowing he was scheduled to meet with the other members of the Millionaires' Club soon to deliver an update, he left his home office as soon as the market closed and drove to meet her at her after-school program. He rounded the corner just as she was finishing her class.

"*P* words," she said, dressed in pink and purple for obvious reasons. She wore a giant pipe cleaner shaped into the letter *P* on her head. Something inside him lightened at the sight of her.

"Pretty!" yelled one little girl.

"Pirate," called a boy.

"Pancake," yelled another.

And so on until Amy held up her hands. "I think

you've got it," she said. "It's time for us to *part*," she said, grinning as she emphasized the last word. "You've been practically perfect. Ask your parents to talk to you about the letter *Q*. Bye for now."

She glanced around the room as the little ones left and her gaze landed on Justin. She met his eyes for a long moment that hit him like a gut punch. He walked toward her.

"You've surprised me again," she said. "Just please tell me you're not having a recurrence of your ulcer."

He shook his head. "I'm still clear," he said, then remembered the original purpose for his visit. "I asked you about your program a few times and what the financial needs were, but you never answered."

She nodded, the *P* pipe cleaner bobbing on her head. "And you never told me why you were interested."

"I know someone who may be interested in helping."

She brightened. "Oh, that would be great. A blank check would be great, too," she joked, then her eyes clouded. "A new social worker would be terrific."

"Ms. Hatcher still causing problems?" he asked.

Amy absently pulled the makeshift *P* hat from her head and sighed. "Every time I think we're making progress, she throws something else in front of me.

I'm starting to wonder if she really can prevent me from adopting the kids.''

Seeing her discouragement, Justin felt an odd need to fix her situation. He shouldn't care, he thought, but for some strange reason he did. "I have some connections. Would a different lawyer help?"

"I think I need to be about ten years older and married," she said wryly. "Got any miracles in your pocket?"

Miracle. The word jarred him. He swallowed over a knot of tension in his throat. Miracles were too closely associated with the man upstairs for Justin's comfort. "So you're saying that if you were either ten years older or married, you would have no problem with gaining custody of the children?"

"Both would be nice," she said. "But either would probably work at the moment."

"You would give up ten years for those kids?" he asked incredulously.

"Oh, yeah," she said without pause. "A stable loving parent during childhood can make all the difference in the world."

She spoke as if she'd experienced a stable loving environment. Justin felt a sliver of envy. "Did yours make a big difference for you?"

She paused and met his gaze. "I didn't have the most stable upbringing. I always viewed my background as something I would overcome, and for the most part, I think I have. I want something different for my sister's children.''

In that moment Justin felt a bone-deep connection that reverberated throughout him like shifting plates of the earth's crust during an earthquake. Justin looked into the fire of Amy's brown eyes and had the sinking sense that he was staring into the face of his purpose.

Three

―――

"No, no and no," Justin muttered as he entered O'Malley's bar later that night. "This has got to be a joke," he said to himself. To God. "I thought we had this settled. You know more than anyone that I am not a choice candidate for marriage or anything involving kids." Continuing his conversation with the Almighty, Justin made his way to the opposite end of the bar where Michael and Dylan were seated. "I realize you're perfect and you don't make mistakes, but this looks like the makings of a whopper to me."

"Justin, who are you talking to?" Dylan asked.

Justin shrugged. "You wouldn't understand."

"Did you get the research taken care of?" Dylan grinned. "I realize how much you hate to part with your green, but we've been talking about the after-school reading program for months."

"I talked to the woman in charge of the program and she gave me a figure. I think it's low, though."

Dylan and Michael stared at him in surprise.

"Low?" Michael echoed. "Does that mean you think we should kick in more?"

Justin nodded. "Yeah, and maybe we can find a ladies' club or something to sponsor the program. It needs some visibility."

Dylan shook his head. "I never thought I'd see the day when you'd suggest we give *more*. I never thought I'd hear the word *more* come out of your mouth in association with giving away your money."

Justin shrugged. Giving away another thirty thousand bucks was the least of his worries at the moment. "Things change."

Dylan frowned. "What's happening with the market lately?"

"It's up and down like it always is. Why?"

"Are you still doing okay with it?"

Better than okay, actually, Justin thought. "Most days," he said. "Why? Do you need a tip?"

"No, you just seem different."

Justin accepted the beer Michael offered him. "I am different. It's not enough for me to make money and hoard it. It never felt right to spend it for the sake of spending.''

"Like me," Dylan said, his eyes glinting with dark challenge. For all his fun and games, Justin knew Dylan had a deeper side.

"Let's just say you haven't had the same hang-ups about spending that I've had," Justin said wryly and took a long swallow of beer.

"I've had more time to spend my inheritance. Up to now, my position on the board of my dear departed father's company has been nonexistent. That's about to change, though," Dylan said, his voice holding a thread of steel.

"What brought this on? The trip to Belize?" Michael asked. "Without Alisa?"

"Belize was great," Dylan said. "No paved roads, not much to do except dive and pet nurse sharks. The breeze blows all the crap from your head. Alisa may be the one that got away, but the seat on the board is mine and it's time I took ownership.''

"Watch out, Remington Pharmaceuticals," Michael said, lifting his bottle in salute. "If you guys would get married and have a kid, your lives would be a helluva lot better. Speaking of which, I've got new baby pictures of Michelle."

Justin and Dylan groaned. "Just because things worked out with you and Kate doesn't mean the rest of us should get married." Dylan elbowed Justin.

"Right? Justin my man is the poster boy for a forever bachelor. Right?"

Justin paused, hearing *M* words ring in his ears like a discordant bell. Miracle. Marriage. There was a reason both came to mind at the same time. As far as Justin could see, a successful marriage took a miracle.

Dylan elbowed him again. "Right?"

"Right," Justin muttered and took another long swallow of beer. He felt Michael's curious gaze on him and had no interest in answering any more questions. "The after-school research is done, so it's your turn with the medical research," he said to Dylan.

"No problem," Dylan said. "Any other business?"

"None from me except Kate wanted me to invite you two for a cookout this weekend."

"Will Alisa be there?" Dylan asked.

"I don't know," Michael said with a shrug. "I thought you said that was over."

"It is," Dylan said in a cold voice.

"Think you can make it?" Michael asked Justin.

"I'll let you know. You never know when a family emergency can crop up."

Michael screwed up his face in confusion. "But you don't have any family."

"Exactly," Justin said, thinking of Amy and her brood. If he ended up with a family, it would defi-

nitely be an emergency. "I've got some charts I
need to check. Later," he said and left the bar knowing his two friends were shaking their heads over
him.

James Bond didn't do the trick tonight. After Justin studied a few stock charts, he tried a DVD, but
his mind kept wandering to Amy. He told himself
he would write a check for the after-school program
and get the best lawyer he could find, but his
thoughts sat on his brain like an undigested meal.
He finally went to bed and after an hour of tossing
and turning, he fell asleep.

The Scrooge dreams returned with Amy's kids
featured as poor and needy. Little Emily never
smiled and the sparkle vanished from the twins'
eyes. Ms. Hatcher played an evil housemother, but
the star fool bore an uncanny resemblance to himself. He was the one who could have changed everything and made life better for Amy and her kids,
but his reluctance kept him from it, and he died before he could change his mind. Desperate to gain
custody of the children, Amy agreed to marry a man
who would kill her spirit.

With sickening horror, Justin watched in Tech-
nicolor as Amy took her vows to such a man. Everything within him rebelled. *No. No.* "No!"

Justin sat straight up in bed, his body in a cold

sweat. The image disturbed him so much his heart pounded with his fury.

Taking several deep breaths, he cleared his head. He rose from the bed, naked, and walked to his window. He pushed aside the curtain and drank in the moonlight.

He wasn't dead. Amy and the kids were still safe. It had only been a dream. Only a dream.

"Yeah, right," Justin muttered and shook his head. This was no dream. This was a kick in the butt. No more running. Justin knew his purpose was clear. Heaven help him, he was supposed to marry Amy.

"You think we should what?" Amy said, unable to believe her ears as she stared at Justin. He'd called her and asked to come over to speak to her after she put the kids to bed. Although she'd been tired, she agreed.

"I think we should get married," Justin said. "You said you needed a husband to get custody of the children. I'm the one you need."

Her stomach took a dip at his words. "But we don't love each other."

"Exactly," he agreed.

"We don't really even like each other."

"I don't agree with that," he said. "I like you."

Amy dipped her head and covered her face with her hand. "I like you. Let's get married," she whispered to herself. She lifted her gaze to his again. "This just doesn't make sense to me. Why would you do this? I mean, you don't need a green card or anything, do you?"

He shook his head. "No. I'm a U.S. citizen," he said, then looked away. "This is hard to explain."

"Try me," she said.

"You know how you have this strong feeling that part of your purpose in life is to help those disadvantaged preschoolers?"

Amy nodded, but the connection eluded her. "Yes."

Justin stood and shoved his hands in his pockets. He walked restlessly to the other side of her den. "Well, when I had that medical emergency, I had a weird dream and I kinda got the message that there was a reason I'm on this earth and I needed to find out what it was."

"And?" she prompted, still not making any connection.

He turned to face her. "I had another weird dream last night. This one was about you and the kids, and I think—" His jaw hardened. "I *know* I'm supposed to marry you."

"Omigoodness," she said, realization sprinkling through her like a cold rain shower. "You think marrying me is your mission."

"I wouldn't say mission," he said, wincing.

"Then what would you call it?"

"The same reason you gave me when you took me to the hospital. You are one of my reasons for being on this planet."

He spoke with such rock-solid certainty that she blinked. She almost believed him. She would have believed him if the notion had not been so totally insane. "Please don't take this the wrong way, but does your family have a history of mental illness?"

His laugh was short and wry. "No. This is more sane than it appears. You need a husband, and I need to keep my deal with the Almighty."

"I didn't make your deal with the Almighty," she pointed out.

"But you made a deal with yourself to get custody of your sister's children and give them a loving home."

He was right, and Amy wasn't sure she liked him for it. "But I don't really need you to keep the deal I made with myself."

Justin just met her glare with an uplifted brow.

"I shouldn't need you," she said, standing and looking up at him. At the moment, she didn't like his height, and she didn't like the strength in his face. She especially didn't like the fact that he seemed far less rattled by this than she did. "I don't know anything about you. I don't know if you have a criminal record."

"I don't."

"I don't know what your education level is," she continued.

"I graduated from St. Albans with a B.S. in Finance."

"I don't know if you have a drinking problem."

"I don't."

His gaze was so open and level she couldn't not believe him. Desperation trickled through her. "Children are very expensive. You may not make good money. I can't afford to feed and house another person."

His eyes flickered with a touch of humor. "I make okay money."

"Children are expensive," she insisted.

"I make very good money," he said, his left eye twitching.

Amy felt a sinking sensation in her stomach. She would bite her tongue in two before she asked the obvious question.

"I'm a millionaire," he finally, reluctantly said.

Stunned, Amy blinked at him. "Pardon?"

"Million, six zeroes," he said.

She sucked in a quick breath. "But you don't look like a millionaire."

His lips twitched. "How does a millionaire look?"

"I don't know," she said, thinking Justin was entirely too attractive. "Bill Gates?"

"He's a billionaire," he said.

"Oh," she said. "Well, when you get up to six zeroes, who's counting?"

"A billion has nine zeroes."

"It doesn't matter," she said, waving her hand and looking at him sideways. "Are you sure you're not a kook?"

He met her with the most level, sane gaze she'd ever seen. "I'm not a kook. I'm proposing marriage because—"

"—it's your mission."

"Because I believe it's one of the reasons I'm here on earth," he said. "As crazy as it sounds, I bet you can respect that."

She could respect it. "Kinda," she agreed and rubbed her eyes. She felt as if she were in some other-worldly zone.

"Saturday okay?"

Amy sighed. "For what?"

"For getting married," he said in a calm voice.

Her eyes flew open. "That's four days away."

"Did you want to do it sooner?" he asked, again in a voice so calm she questioned his sanity.

Her heart shot into her throat. "No!" She shook her head. "I don't know if I can do this. I don't know if it's a good idea. I'm going to have to think about it."

"That's okay," he said. "I had a tough time with it at first, too."

She eyed him curiously. "What did you do?"

"Shook my head, said no a lot, broke out in a cold sweat."

"You don't look at all upset now," she said, and barely kept the accusation from her voice.

"It's right," he said. "I never thought I would say that, but it is." He leaned forward and squeezed her arm. "Sleep on it, but remember Ms. Hatcher."

"I'll never sleep if I think about Ms. Hatcher."

"I can make her go away," he said in a voice liquid with sensual promise.

Amy felt something inside her shift and quiver. That last statement was the most seductive offer she'd had in ages. Talk about a dream come true. Make Ms. Hatcher go away. "I'll think about it," she told him.

"Name the date," he said as if they could have been meeting for bagels and coffee. "And I'll get it done."

His casual tone belied the formidable look in his eyes, letting Amy know he would accomplish anything he set out to do.

"G'night," he said, and brushed his fingers over her cheek before he walked out the door.

Her cheek burning from his touch, she lifted her hand to cradle it as she watched him walk to his car. A swirl of emotions spun her head round and round. She had joked about needing a husband to pass muster with Ms. Hatcher, but it had been strictly a joke. Or so she'd thought.

All her experiences with Justin had been odd from the beginning. He'd proposed marriage when she had thought a date with him would be nice. Her head began to throb. How could he be so calm? Surely he must be insane.

Pushing away from the doorjamb, she pinched the bridge of her nose. She had never pictured herself married. Then again, she hadn't pictured herself mothering her sister's three children either. Locking the door, she walked down the hall and peeked in on the twins. Jeremy's covers were already kicked off and his thumb was tucked in his mouth. Nick slept on his tummy with his mouth open.

In sleep their rowdiness quieted and they looked so sweetly vulnerable. Amy's heart caught. They'd lost so much at such a young age, she thought, feeling the grief from her sister's death wash over her.

Amy tiptoed to Jeremy's bed and pulled up the covers. She leaned down and gave him the softest breath of a kiss. He sighed, and she smiled.

Leaving the room, she closed the door behind her to check on Emily. Everything inside her tightened at the sight of the little girl. Emily clutched an old stuffed teddy bear in her hands. She was old enough to have a better idea of what she'd lost. Amy could tell Emily wanted so badly to please. Emily tried very hard to act like an adult, as if she could handle anything. It was almost as if she was afraid to cry,

Amy thought, as if she didn't trust the security of her situation enough to relax.

Amy kneeled beside Emily's bed and gently stroked the little girl's forehead. Although the idea chafed at her feminist conscience, Amy suspected Emily would benefit from a man around the house. The solidity and security offered by the right man could work wonders. But was Justin the right man? Amy wondered.

An image of Ms. Hatcher flashed through her mind, sending a cold chill through her. Amy frowned. These children needed her. They needed her love and stability, and they needed to belong to her.

Amy thought again of Justin's proposal.

A long, long time ago, when she was much younger, she had dreamed of finding a man to love, a man who would provide a safe harbor from the bad stuff life threw at her or him. Then she grew up and realized she had to make her own safe harbor, her own security; and needing a man could actually make her more vulnerable instead of less.

Long before Amy became an adult, she'd preferred to pilot her own ship. The idea of sharing the helm unsettled her. It wouldn't be her top choice.

She glanced again at Emily as she lay sweetly sleeping. Emily hadn't gotten her top choice either, Amy thought, her sister's death weighing heavily on her shoulders. Justin's proposal dangled before her, alternately seducing and repelling her.

Justin's phone rang at 6:00 a.m. Amy wanted to meet him after the kids left. She had called the school and arranged to go in late. Justin pulled into her driveway behind her Volkswagen and threaded his way through the obstacle course of Big Wheel toys on the walkway to her porch. Glancing at his watch, he rang the doorbell. He hoped to make it back to his house in time for the opening of the market. If he was going to bear some responsibility for three children, he was going to need to continue to make money.

Three children. His stomach turned. Heaven help him. Heaven had better help him, he thought, because this sure as hell hadn't been his idea.

Amy greeted him at the door, her gaze wary, her smile absent. The thought struck him that he would have liked to see her smile. She led him into the den and waved her hand at the sofa.

Justin sat. She didn't. She paced, the hem of her flippy skirt emphasizing the length of her bare legs.

"There are too many unanswered questions about your pro—" She faltered. "—suggestion that we marry."

He noticed she couldn't cough up the word proposal. If he'd had any secret romantic fantasies about marriage, he supposed he would have had a tough time with it, too. The only fantasy Justin had ever had about marriage was avoiding it. But since this was the deal from the big guy upstairs, Justin had no choice.

"What questions?"

"Where we'll live, how long we'll remain married, if you like children," she said, looking at him sideways. "I have a feeling you don't."

Justin shifted in his seat. "I don't dislike children. I haven't spent much time around them. As to where we'll live—"

"We need to live here," she said. "The kids don't need any further disruption in their lives. They've been through enough."

He nodded slowly. "I'll need a room for an office."

"I have an extra bedroom," she said and took a deep breath. "If we decide to get mar—" She stumbled over the words and shook her head. "If we decide to do this, I think we should do it for two years, then decide if we want to go our separate ways."

Justin turned the terms over in his head. "That's fine. I can get a prenup worked up to provide for you and the kids."

Amy looked at him in horror. "Oh, no! I wouldn't expect alimony or child support once this was over."

He shrugged. "I think that would be best."

She stared at him a long moment and realization crossed her face. "Oh, because it's your mission?"

Her choice of words grated on him. Amy had the kind of voice that could bring men age three to ninety-three to their knees. And her body— Justin wasn't on his knees, but he damn well wouldn't deny she aroused a distinctly *un*mission-like response in him. "One of the reasons I was put on earth," he corrected.

She nodded. "Okay. I think we need to keep the surprises to a minimum, so you need to know that I'm very independent and I don't take orders or interference well at all."

"That doesn't surprise me," he said, thinking of Amy's interplay with Ms. Hatcher. "I'm not interested in interfering or giving orders. I'm here to provide you with a vehicle to get custody of your sister's children and financial assistance."

She gave a quick nod and looked at him uneasily.

"What else?" Justin asked, impatient.

She crossed her arms under her breasts. "We need to discuss sex."

Four

Justin went completely silent. In odd random moments when he hadn't been fighting the idea that this marriage would likely kill him financially, if not mentally, he'd thought about taking Amy to bed. It was no hardship to imagine her lithe legs wrapped around his hips and her full breasts massaging his chest while he thrust inside her. She lived her life so passionately he'd like to see how that passion translated in the bedroom.

Her brown eyes wide with a mixture of uncertainty and a sliver of forbidden curiosity, she twisted her fingers together. Despite her bravado, Justin saw the vulnerability underneath. ''You've thought about sex?'' he asked, rising to his feet. It occurred to him that his sanity could well be pushed to the brink living in such close proximity to Amy and not taking her for his own.

She bit her lip. ''Uh, kinda, well, not really,'' she quickly amended. ''You can sleep in the extra bedroom. It can double as your office.''

Justin studied her for a long moment. ''We can change that later.''

Relief washed over her face. ''Yes. Right, later. I mean, we haven't even gone out on a date. I don't know you. You don't know me. We may not want each other,'' she finished in an uncharacteristically breathless voice. She looked at him as if she'd just told the biggest whopper of a lie and prayed he wouldn't call her on it.

Amy looked as if she'd just offered the biggest dare in the world and wanted to call it back. Justin wondered if the seductive images of sharing a bed with him ever danced across her mind. He knew from her covert, fleeting glances at his body that she was aware of him as a man. If she hadn't felt she needed to save her sister's children and then save the rest of the world, he suspected she might just let herself go. Even Amy must struggle with her needs.

He walked toward her and touched her chin. ''You're a beautiful woman,'' he told her. ''I want you. You want me.''

Her eyes widened and she swallowed audibly. "That's a little arrogant, don't you think?"

He shook his head. "It's not arrogance when it's the truth. You have a body that could stop and rewind the clock of every man in St. Albans."

Amy felt the tiniest ripple of pleasure, but told herself not to be flattered. "There are lots of bodies."

"Yes, but not all move like yours," he said.

He'd noticed the way she walked. By the look in his green gaze, he'd noticed quite a bit more. Her heart skipped.

"You have a fire inside you. It shows in your eyes, in your voice, in lots of ways. Men have always liked to play with fire."

The visual of Justin, naked, touching her, made her feel suddenly hot. Before she knew it, he lowered his head and pressed his mouth over hers. He rubbed his lips from side to side, then slid his tongue inside. She was both shocked and mesmerized by his boldness. He kissed her as if he were opening the doors and windows to a house that had been shut for months. For years?

Amy felt a dangerous delicious temptation to lean closer, to feel the sensation of his hard chest against her breasts, to feel more of him. Her heart hammered. Her mind scrambled. This was crazy. Too crazy for today. She had more important things to do, she told herself. The motivation for his proposal to marry washed over her like a cool spray from Nick's water gun. She pushed away.

"*This* is not the reason you want to marry me," she said. "Technically, you don't even want to marry me," she reminded him and herself. "You want to marry me because you think it's your mission."

"One of the reasons I was put on the earth," he corrected in a curt voice, his eyes as turbulent as her emotions.

"Whatever," she said. "You didn't suggest we marry because of your overwhelming love and passion for me. I won't pretend that you did."

"Just as your agreement to marry me is not based on your feeling that you can't live without me," he said.

"I haven't agreed."

"You haven't? Who's pretending now?"

Amy scowled. At the moment, she didn't like him. She didn't like him at all for being right. "All right, dammit, I'll marry you. For the children. I may be a little attracted to you, but that doesn't mean I'm interested in going to bed with you," she said, and tamped down her loud protesting inner voice of truth. "I have my priorities straight here. I'd appreciate it if you'd do the same. I'm not marrying you to save me or take care of me. I learned a long time ago to do that for myself."

His eyes darkened. "Then we're well-matched. I learned the same lesson."

A dozen questions flitted through her mind. What had forced Justin to learn the same hard lesson she had? She burned to ask.

Justin glanced at his watch. "Speaking of priorities, I need to go. The market opens in fifteen minutes. When do you want to get married?"

Her head spun with his businesslike tone. "I'm not sure. Friday or Saturday," she said. "Or next week," she added at the same time she knew the sooner she did the deed, the sooner she would gain custody.

"I'd rather not do it during market hours," Justin said.

Amy nodded. She may never have envisioned herself as Cinderella, but this was a little chilly for even her. "Saturday, then," she said, grimly reminding herself this was for two years. She would do just about anything for two years to keep her sister's children safe.

"Saturday. I'll be in touch," he said and walked out the door.

Amy could have sworn she felt the weight of a noose settle around her neck.

Amy and Justin met downtown for blood tests and to make application for the marriage license. Before she knew it, Saturday arrived. Amy broke into a sweat. *What was she doing!*

Emily knocked on Amy's bedroom door and bounded into the room. She jumped onto Amy's bed, her eyes sparkling with excitement. "We're getting married today!"

Amy gulped and mustered a smile. "Yes, we are."

"Do you want me to make pancakes for breakfast?"

Amy's stomach shrank at the thought. "Oh, that's a lovely offer, but I'm so excited I don't think I could eat." Excited wasn't the most accurate word choice, but Amy refused to quibble with herself this morning. "Could you make pancakes another time?"

Emily dimpled. "Yeah, when Justin moves in."

Amy's stomach twisted. "Right. Great idea," she said and rose from the bed. "You chose your dress last night and the boys' clothes are laid out on their beds. How would you like your hair?"

"Ponytail," Emily said. "With a ribbon?"

"Can do," Amy said, grabbing a brush from the bureau.

Emily stood in front of her staring into the mirror as Amy brushed her hair. "Are you going to wear a long white dress like my Barbie doll has?"

What to wear had been the last thing on her mind. "Uh, no, sweetie. People who wear long dresses have usually planned their weddings a long time in advance.''

"Longer than a week?" Amy said.

Try four days, Amy thought. "Exactly."

"Then what are you going to wear?"

Amy still didn't know. Her brain felt as if it were playing hopscotch. Guessing at Justin's ring size, she'd bought his gold band yesterday. She'd ordered a few flowers from the florist which she planned to pick up on her way to the judge's chambers. She hoped ice cream and the sheet cake she'd bought from the bakery would distract the children from the lack of true emotion surrounding the occasion.

Emily tugged on her sleeve. "What are you going to wear?"

Still at a loss, Amy smiled. "A surprise," she said, and it would be a surprise to herself, too.

"This is what you call a family emergency?" Dylan asked as he entered the hall outside the judge's chambers.

"Any wedding would be to me," Justin said. He'd spent most of the night arguing with the Almighty, trying to convince Him that Justin was not a good choice for this job. It was the strangest coincidence. The thunderstorm had gotten louder and louder the more Justin had argued. When he finally shut up in defeat, so had the storm.

Coincidence, he told himself again, but he knew what he had to do. Marry Amy Monroe.

"I still don't understand this. You made a deal with God." Dylan shook his head. "Are you sure they didn't mess up your anesthesia during your emergency surgery? Maybe your brain was affected—"

"You're here to be a witness," Justin said. "If there's one thing I don't need right now, it's a psychoanalysis from St. Albans's *numero uno* babe magnet."

"Okay, but I have to ask, are you sure she isn't marrying you for your money?"

"I told you. This is not about money. It's about custody." He glanced up and felt a slight easing at the sight of Michael and his wife, Kate.

Michael wore an expression of subdued admiration. "You sure know how to take the fuss out of a wedding. No church, no reception."

"Cheap," Kate added with disapproval.

"Expedient," Justin said, grinding his teeth. "Thank you for coming."

"Oh, my goodness!" Kate said as Amy rounded the corner balancing a bouquet, and holding a hand of each twin. Dressed in a pink frilly dress with a slightly lopsided ponytail, Emily brought up the rear with a miniature bouquet.

Justin's heart stopped. Amy was dressed in a cream-colored lace dress that whispered and sighed over her curves with a hem that kissed her shapely calves. Her hair was pulled up in a topknot with a spray of baby's breath, but a few unruly curls escaped. Her cheeks flushed, she gnawed on her bottom lip in nervousness. She was his bride. The knowledge filled him with surprising warmth.

"The children are adorable," Kate whispered.

Dylan cleared his throat. "Why didn't you tell me she was—"

Justin blinked. "Was what?"

Dylan shrugged. "Well, hell, she's stacked better than the City Library. I gotta tell you," he said with a nudge. "This marriage may not be such a hardship after all."

He had no idea, Justin thought. Amy's gaze finally landed on him, skimming over him from head to toe, then returning to his eyes. If her eyes could talk, they would have said "Are we insane?"

He walked toward her. "You look beautiful," he said, instinctively taking her chilled hand in his.

"Thank you," she said, her gaze dropping to his shirt collar. "You look very nice, too."

He sensed she was trying to hide her apprehension.

"Emily helped," she said.

"You look pretty, too," he said to the little girl.

Emily grinned hugely. "Do you like our flowers?"

"They're almost as pretty as you."

"I gotta go to the bathroom," Nicholas said, shifting from one foot to the other.

Jeremy tugged at his collar. "Aunt Amy says we get cake and ice cream when we get home."

Amy gave a pained smile. "The reward system at work."

"Good idea for the kids."

"And me," she muttered. "I should take Nicholas before we have an accident."

"Let Justin take him," Kate interjected, stepping forward. "I'm Kate Hawkins. This is my husband, Michael, and friend, Dylan. Why don't you guys take the other two children for a drink of water at the fountain while I help the bride?"

Michael's face crinkled in confusion. "Help the bride do what?"

Kate rolled her eyes. "Get ready for the ceremony."

"The ceremony won't take five minutes, so—"

"Sweetheart, would you please take the children to get a drink at the water fountain?"

He blinked. "Sure. Come on," he said to the kids.

Nicholas shifted again. "I gotta go."

Amy didn't want an accident. "So should I."

Justin surprised her by stepping forward and taking Nick's hand. "I'll take him."

Amy paused in surprise. "Are you sure you know how—"

Justin lifted an eyebrow. "I think we can muddle through."

She watched them leave. "It may sound crazy, but I have a hard time believing Justin has ever helped a three-year-old visit the bathroom."

"Given his aversion to children, I'd be surprised, too," Kate said.

"Aversion?" Amy echoed, swerving to look at Kate. The slim brunette with curious warm eyes wore an easy air of sophistication.

Kate gave a wry grin. "That was pre-emergency surgery Justin. He seems to have changed. Some," she added grudgingly. "Would you like one last dash to the powder room?"

Amy nodded and walked toward the ladies' room. "So what was the pre-emergency surgery Justin like?"

"Ultracareful. I always got the impression he had no intention of ever getting married or having children."

Amy's stomach began to twist and turn. "He doesn't like children?"

"I can't say that," Kate said. "He's crazy about our baby, Michelle." She sighed. "These three guys have hidden depths. Maybe it has something to do with spending all that time at the Granger Home for Boys. Maybe—"

Amy's jaw dropped. "Justin lived at the Granger Home for Boys?"

Kate nodded, saving the bouquet from Amy's limp hand. "Oh, yes. All three of them lived there. You didn't know?"

Amy shook her head, trying to make sense of the new information. It reinforced her feeling that there was more to him than what he had revealed. If he'd lived at Granger then he had firsthand experience with the reason Amy wanted custody of the children and why she felt so strongly about making a safe place for them.

"But you know he trades stocks and is very successful at it?" Kate asked.

"Yes. When he suggested that we get married, I told him I couldn't afford another mouth to feed and he told me he was a millionaire."

"This has happened so fast I bet he didn't have time to get you to sign a prenup," Kate said, extremely amused by the idea.

"I signed it the same afternoon we got our blood taken. It was more than generous." She met Kate's gaze. "I'm not interested in his money." She hesitated revealing her feelings. "I'm marrying Justin to ease the process for gaining custody of the children. To be perfectly honest, I've never set my sights on marrying any man, let alone a rich man. It always appeared to me that a woman pays in self-esteem and autonomy for that decision."

Kate stared at her in surprise, then smiled. "I think you may be very good for Justin."

Looking in the mirror, Amy felt a swirl of contradicting emotions. In less than fifteen minutes, she would be a wife. "This marriage may not last long," she confessed in a whisper.

Kate gave her a considering glance. "Michael and I didn't marry under the best circumstances and I didn't think our marriage would last."

"You changed your mind?"

Kate smiled. "Michael changed my mind. For what it's worth, Michael says Justin is a stand-up guy. When the chips are down and everyone else has fallen, Justin is the one who'll still be standing by you."

That sounded so incredibly tempting to Amy. Sometimes she felt she'd spent her life being the stand-up woman. Her palms damp, she rubbed them on the sides of her dress. *For the children,* she repeated to herself like a mantra. She licked her lips. "I guess it's time."

Kate looked at her with sympathy in her eyes. "We'd already planned a cookout this afternoon. Why don't we let it double as a wedding party?"

"I already have cake and ice cream at home for the kids," Amy said.

"Bring it," Kate said. "Hey, it's one less meal you'll have to cook. And my little girl will worship your children because they can walk and run."

"Thanks for the offer. Let's get through the ceremony first," Amy said, feeling an overwhelming urge to hike up her dress and run.

"It'll be short," Kate told her in a reassuring tone as she returned the bouquet. "You look beautiful."

Amy and Kate left the ladies' room and encountered the rest of the group in the hallway. Justin caught Amy's eye and strode to her side. "Ready?"

No. She nodded.

"I'm not an axe murderer," he assured her. "Just for my own peace of mind, you're not related to Lorena Bobbit, that woman who cut off her husband's..."

Amy almost laughed. "No. Did everything go okay with Nick?"

"No problem. Just unzipped and put him in front of the urinal and let it fly."

Amy felt a tug on her dress and looked down to find Nick smiling broadly. "Justin showed me a new way to pee. It's a lot better than sitting. Jeremy wants to try it now."

Amy looked up at Justin. "Thank you for your contribution. I think," she added.

"It was nothing," he said. "Guy-thing. You ready?"

No, but I'd really like to get it over with. "Let's do it," she said gamely and walked into the judge's chambers.

Judge Bishop, a friendly man in his fifties, had just arrived from a morning golf game, jubilant over his score. "This is a great day to get married," he said as he was introduced to Amy. "I shot a score of sixty-eight and left the rest of my foursome in the dust."

Amy pushed her lips into a smile, wondering if she would remember that little tidbit in years to come.

"I'll keep this short, so you can get to the good stuff," Judge Bishop said with a broad wink.

Amy felt her smile falter. Oxygen was suddenly in short supply. Justin continued to hold her hand.

"Do you take this man…" the judge began, and Amy feared she might hyperventilate. Out of desperation, she did something she rarely did except for children. She pretended. She pretended she was talking to an order taker at Burger Doodle.

"…to have and to hold from this day forward for richer and poorer…"

Amy translated, *Do you want mustard and pickles on your burger?*

"I do," she whispered.

"In sickness and in health…"

Do you want fries with that?

"I do," she whispered again.

"Till death do you part?"

And a hot apple pie?

"I do," she said, firmly aloud.

From the corner of her mind, she heard Justin answer the same way she had. The bubble surrounding her game of pretend began to deflate when the judge asked for the rings. Emily bounced to her side with Justin's ring attached to a ribbon on her little nosegay.

With trembling fingers, Amy pushed the band on Justin's finger and repeated the words, "With this ring, I thee wed."

She stared at the wide gold band with the diamond solitaire Justin placed on her third finger and heard his voice repeat the same words. The weight of it was unfamiliar. The metal felt cold against her skin. She was enormously glad she wouldn't have to say anything else because she was too stunned by the ring to make a sound. The ring was definitely not a cheeseburger with mustard and pickles, fries and an apple pie.

She glanced up to find him staring at his own gold band in shock.

"You may now kiss the bride," the judge said.

Justin met her gaze and she had the slipping, sliding feeling that she had just danced with fate, done the polka with eternity. Though she may have pretended it, those were not Burger Doodle vows she'd just made.

Justin lowered his mouth to hers, and all her pretending was over.

Five

Amy felt as if she'd spent the day at the circus, minus the fun. After the ceremony, everyone met at the Hawkins's for a barbecue. The children enjoyed themselves immensely and Amy relaxed a tad until Dylan gave a second toast. It was definitely time to leave. The children were on such a sugar high from the cake and ice cream that they skipped their afternoon naps and "helped" Justin move in.

She prepared a gourmet dinner of peanut butter and jelly sandwiches and chicken noodle-o's soup. God finally smiled on her when all the kids tuckered out early and she put them to bed. Leaning against the wall in the darkened hallway, she closed her eyes and let out a long sigh. The only sounds she heard were the faint ticking of the downstairs clock and the rustling of computer and modem cords as Justin continued to set up his office.

She rubbed her thumb over the still unfamiliar wide gold band on her finger. Needing solitude, but unwilling to go to her bedroom just yet, she walked downstairs and lay down on the sofa in the quiet den.

Moments later, Justin appeared in the doorway. A dark silhouette with broad shoulders, he emanated a quiet strength merely by his presence. Amy wondered if the strength was in her imagination. There was so much she didn't know about him.

"One question," he said, his voice low and intimate in the darkness. "With those kids helping, how do you get anything done?"

She smiled at the dismay in his voice. "The rule of thumb is if you're female, you add an hour to your estimated completion time for every child helping you."

He strolled toward her and looked down at her. "And if you're male?"

"Add eight," Amy said.

"Eight?"

Amy nodded, keeping her head on the pillow. "Eight for every child helping you. It's unfortunate, but men have difficulty focusing on more than one thing at a time. I'm not sure if it's due to hormones or the Y chromosome.''

''Where did you learn this fun fact?''

''Oh, it's well known. Ask any married mother.'' She took a breath and looked up at him, a male stranger in her house. Her husband. Her heart jumped. She closed her eyes, thinking he might not affect her so much if she didn't look at him. ''Is part of the reason you offered to marry me because you once lived at the Granger Home for Boys?''

''Kate's been talking.''

''A little,'' Amy said, wondering why his voice felt like it rubbed over her like a forbidden caress. ''It wasn't all bad. You didn't answer my question.''

''My experience at Granger may have influenced me, but it wasn't the deciding factor.''

''Your *mission* was the deciding factor,'' she said, reminding herself as much as him.

Feeling his hand close around her ankle, she opened her eyes in surprise.

''Do I have your attention?'' he asked.

''Yes, and my foot.''

''Good,'' he said, not releasing her ankle. ''If we're going to live together, we need to come to an understanding about a few things.''

The slow motion of his thumb on the inside of her ankle distracted her. ''What things?''

''Your annoying description of why I proposed to

you," he said, holding firm when she wiggled her foot.

"Mission," she said. "What's wrong with that?"

"I said it was part of my purpose," he corrected through gritted teeth.

"Semantics. Would you let go of my foot?"

"When we reach our understanding," he said. His thumb and middle finger formed a human ankle cuff. The sight of his hand on her bare skin disrupted her.

"You want me to call it your purpose," she said.

"That would be better."

"We understand each other," she said, noticing that his finger began its mesmerizing motion again. "You can let go of my foot."

"Not quite," he said. "We don't understand each other yet. We don't know each other."

Amy gave a little test jerk of her foot to no avail. "Your point?"

"We don't have to make this situation a living hell for each other."

She met his gaze, wondering how one of his fingers could make her insides turn to warm liquid. "And how do we accomplish that?"

"We get to know each other," he said in a voice that brought to mind hot nights and tangled sheets.

She wanted to say she didn't have time to get to know him, but he chose that moment to skim a fingertip up the sole of her foot. Her stomach dipped.

"For the sake of peace of mind," he said.

She searched her mind for a reason to disagree, but her brain had turned to sludge. "Okay."

"We start tonight. I ask you a question and then you ask me one."

"Truth or dare," Amy said, not at all sure this was a good idea.

"Just truth," Justin said.

"Okay, ladies first," she said, shifting into a more upright position, ready to ask the question that had been burning a hole in her mind all day. "How did you end up at Granger?"

His jaw tightened. "My mother was unable to care for me."

"Why?" she asked.

He shook his head. "That's two," he said. "My turn. The first time I met you I asked you to dinner. If you hadn't been caring for your sister's children, what would your answer have been?"

Amy squirmed slightly. It was much more fun asking questions than answering them. "Gosh, that was a long time ago, almost two months ago. And I got pretty distracted when you had the ulcer attack," she said, trying to lead him away from his original question.

"What would your answer have been?"

Amy made a face. "Maybe."

"Your answer would have been maybe," he said. Amy frowned at his disbelieving voice. How had he known she'd been intrigued by him from the beginning? "Okay," she admitted. "Maybe yes."

"I'm not familiar with what 'maybe yes' means. I'm sure it's my Y chromosome. Could you translate?" he asked, massaging her ankle.

Amy glowered at him. "It means yes. You were interested in my after-school program. How could I resist?" she rhetorically asked. She told herself she'd been completely unaffected by his watchful, intelligent green eyes, chiseled facial features and those broad shoulders that looked like they could carry any problem a woman might face. Amy wondered why she felt as if she were back in pretending land again.

He nodded and released her foot. Her ankle felt surprisingly bereft. "Sleep tight, Amy," he said and turned to leave.

Oddly miffed, she sprang up from the couch. "Sleep tight? That's it?"

He glanced around at her with one lifted eyebrow. "I stuck to my proposal. One question," he said. "Did you want something else?"

His voice was like a velvet invitation over her skin. The way he looked at her reminded her she was a woman. She fought the urge to rub away the effect of his touch on her ankle. She crossed her arms over her chest and shook her head. "No. G'night."

After watching him leave the room, she stood

there for several moments, trying to regain her calm, but it had vanished like Houdini. She climbed the stairs and entered her bedroom, stripped and pulled on a cotton nightshirt. As she climbed into bed, Amy tried not to think about the fact that a dark, masculine stranger lay just down the hall from her, and that the dark masculine stranger was her husband.

Justin lay in a lumpy bed in a room one half the size of his walk-in closet. His *bride,* who possessed a body designed to make him burn with lust every wretched night of his immediate future, lay approximately twenty-five feet away. He hoped God was very happy.

Justin was waiting for the peace he'd expected in exchange for fulfilling at least the initial phase of his purpose on earth. Instead, when he closed his eyes, he saw Amy sprawled out on the sofa downstairs, her hair a riot, her eyes filled with sensual curiosity. Even her ankles got to him, slim, creamy and delicate. He had wanted to trace his finger up her calf to the inside of her thigh and higher still.

Justin wondered if hell could possibly be worse than being married to a woman who resented you and needed you at the same time. He stifled a groan. Then he thought of the kids and the tight feeling in his chest eased slightly. Even though they were nosey, noisy and expensive, he wouldn't wish his upbringing on them. He admired Amy for her commitment and sacrifice. In a strange way, their shared goal bound them together.

All fine and good, he thought as he rolled over on the soft mattress, but he wondered if the next two years would drive him quietly insane and totally broke. That image kept him awake for hours.

Justin finally drifted into a dreamless sleep. A sound permeated his deep slumber. He buried his head further in the pillow, but the sound persisted. It wrenched at something deep inside him before he even identified it.

A child was crying. Justin sat upright and listened. "Nick."

Hustling out of bed, he ran into the hall and collided with Amy. He instinctively closed his arms around her when she began to fall. She gasped, and he dimly noted her breasts heaving pleasurably against his chest. Her fingers closed around his biceps.

"Omigod, are you naked?" she whispered.

"Boxers," he said, feeling the brush of her thighs against his. Nick let out another sob that would rip the heart from Atilla the Hun. "Nick's crying."

"I know," she whispered, disentangling herself. "He does this every few nights. It used to be every night. I think it's part of his way of working out his grief. I'll take care of it."

She carefully opened the door and moved quickly to his side. Quietly following, Justin watched her touch his arm and whisper to him. "It's okay, baby."

"Aunt Amy?" he asked in a husky voice, giving a hiccup.

"It's me," she said, stroking his face. "You're okay."

"I had a scary dream. I was at Chica's Pizza and everybody left me. I was all by myself and I couldn't find you."

"That's not gonna happen," she said. "You're stuck with me. Do you want to get a drink of water and use the bathroom?"

He nodded. "Can I pee the way Justin taught me?"

Justin smothered a chuckle and stepped forward. "Yep, and I'll help," he said, offering his hand to Nick.

Catching Amy's look of surprise, Justin guided the wobbly child to the bathroom and held him up so he could drink from the faucet, then helped him finish with the toilet. He returned the boy to Amy.

"He has never shown this much motivation to use the bathroom," Amy murmured.

"That Y chromosome comes in handy when you least expect it."

She shook her head, but smiled. "I'll tuck him in."

"What about me?" he asked, figuring he could blame his audacity on the late hour.

"What about you?" she asked.

"When are you going to tuck me in?" he asked. "It's my first night here. I might have a bad dream."

"Count sheep," she said.

Justin wondered how such a woman who was so warm and generous with the kids could be so heartless with him. He knew, however, that Amy resented needing him to accomplish her goal.

And so began the inauspicious, passionless marriage of Amy and Justin. The following day was a flurry of activity with Justin continuing to get *help* from the children setting up his computer. The boys fastened themselves to him like glue, and in the corner of her mind, Amy wondered about them growing attached to him.

That evening, he met her again in the den. This time she was ready for him. She crossed her legs Indian style so he wouldn't work his voodoo on her ankle again. "Why couldn't your mother take care of you? Was she sick?"

He walked behind the couch and touched her hair. She turned her head to look at him.

"She wasn't physically ill," he said. "Or mentally ill in the true sense. She just couldn't manage money. Every month she would receive a check for child support from my father and she would spend it all within three days. Bills piled up, the landlord threw us out, our electricity was cut off too many times to count. She would stay out all night sometimes. A neighbor found out and called social services. Not long after that, I started living at Granger.''

Her heart twisted at the picture he'd drawn of his childhood. Amy's upbringing may not have been a fairy tale, but her mother was usually around even if she'd passed out drunk more nights than not.

''Neglect,'' she murmured. ''How old were—''

He shook his head. ''—one question. My turn. What made you decide you wanted to change the world?''

Her lips twitched. More than one friend had teased her for her crusader orientation. ''I don't have to change the world, really,'' she said. ''Although that would be nice. I can just be satisfied working on my little corner of it.''

Justin shrugged. ''You didn't answer my question. What made you decide—''

Amy waved her hand. ''Okay. When I was about thirteen or fourteen, I observed that there were two kinds of people in the world. People who make a difference and people who waste their lives. I saw too many people waste their lives to know I didn't want that for myself.''

She could see the follow-up questions on his face, but he just nodded. ''Okay, good night.''

The same irritation spiced with indignation she'd felt last night prickled through her. He clearly had more control and less curiosity than she did, blast him. "Good night," she said, trying to keep the edge from her voice.

Justin glanced over his shoulder. "It'll be a helluva lot better for both of us when you stop being angry that you accepted my help. Sleep tight," he said and climbed the stairs.

Amy gaped after him. *Angry! Me, angry?* She had half a mind to chase him up those stairs and show him what *angry* was. While it may be true that she was exasperated with the legal system, and she resented the fact that getting married would make it easier to gain custody of the children, she wasn't angry with Justin. She wasn't pleased she'd had to marry a stranger, and the marriage was turning her life upside down, but her anger was directed at lawyers and a certain social worker. Not Justin. Right.

Monday presented the usual problems associated with the first day of the week. Justin left early saying he would work at his home during market hours until he got the kinks out of his new computer system. Emily missed the school bus, Nick had an accident, and when Amy arrived at school, she faced a class with so many children sick from a virus her classroom should have been quarantined.

That evening Justin didn't arrive home by dinnertime, making Amy wonder if he was experiencing buyer's remorse. Probably sensing her edginess, the kids chose that night for a full-fledged arsenic hour.

Topping it off with a cherry, Ms. Hatcher arrived at the door. Amy just managed to beat Emily to the door. Moving her lips into what she hoped looked like a smile, Amy opened the door and greeted the woman.

"Good evening, Ms. Hatcher. Do come in. You've arrived just at dinner time again," Amy said, cheerfully trying to keep the edge from her voice.

"I nearly tripped over the tricycle on the sidewalk," Ms. Hatcher grumbled as they headed away from the foyer.

"I'm so sorry," Amy said, thinking it was a shame the woman hadn't broken her neck. As soon as the thought whispered across her mind, she winced, hoping she wouldn't get struck by lightning. "I wish I could offer you dessert, but—"

Amy heard the front door open and close. She glanced past Ms. Hatcher to see Justin. Her stomach flipped. She and Justin hadn't prepared for this. She didn't know whether to kiss him or tell him to leave. A visit from Ms. Hatcher was too important to muddle, and she and Justin hadn't even made plans. "Justin," she said, biting her lip, "Ms. Hatcher is here."

"Hi, Justin!" the twins chorused.

Waving to the boys, he quickly surveyed the

scene and walked toward Amy. "Nice to see you, Ms. Hatcher. Has Amy had a chance to share our news with you?"

The woman frowned as Justin put his arm around Amy. "News? What news?"

"We were married over the weekend. You can be among the first to congratulate us."

Ms. Hatcher's eyes nearly popped out of her head. "You're married? So quickly?"

He nuzzled Amy's hair, surprising the dickens out of her. "When it's right, it's best not to wait. Amy and I have each other, and the children have two parents."

"B-b-but, what about your honeymoon?"

Amy stiffened.

Justin skimmed his fingers down the sensitive inside of her arm and laced his long fingers through hers. "I'd like nothing more than to have my bride all to myself, but we thought it would be much better for the children not to leave them for a while." He squeezed Amy's hand a little too tightly as if to wake her from a trance. "Right, sweetheart?"

Amy nodded. "Right. The children have really taken to Justin, and I think it will be wonderful for both the boys and Emily to have a successful male role model in the home." Amy resisted the urge to put her finger down her throat. Give her pearls, heels and a vacuum cleaner and she could have been a 1950s television wife.

"Well, we will need to interview Mr. Langdon and perform our routine check," Ms. Hatcher said, clearly still struggling with her surprise.

Amy battled another dart of anxiety. What if there was something detrimental in Justin's past?

"Feel free. It's important for you to do your job," Justin said and to Amy's ears he might as well have said "Have at it, you nosey hag. I have nothing to hide."

She needed to get Ms. Hatcher out the door. She wouldn't be able to sustain the 1950s television wife persona much longer. "Was there anything else you needed this evening?" she asked.

"Not that I can think—"

"Then let me escort you to the door," Justin said. Amy wondered if he'd noticed her squeaky tone of voice. She suspected he knew how tense she was.

He deliberately pried Amy's fingers from his and took Ms. Hatcher's arm.

"Thank you," she said under her breath and felt her shoulder twitch when the woman turned away. A moment later, it twitched again.

Emily looked at her curiously. "Aunt Amy, why are you moving your arm funny?"

"I don't know, sweetie," she said, rolling her shoulder. "I think I'm a little tense." *Or maybe I'm allergic to Ms. Hatcher.*

Justin returned and met Amy's gaze. "She's gone."

Amy heaved a sigh of relief and rushed toward him. She impulsively hugged him and pressed her mouth against his, then pulled backed. ''I cannot tell you how much I appreciate you showing up at the exact moment you did. Thank you. Thank you. I owe you a big one.''

Justin glanced down her body with a sensual once-over, then seared her from the inside out with a warm, yet challenging gaze. ''How big a one do you owe me?''

Oops. Amy felt her heart skip. She wondered if she'd traded the Wicked Witch of the West, Ms. Hatcher, for the Big Bad Wolf, her husband.

Six

Amy felt a tugging sensation on her shorts. She glanced down at Jeremy.

"What's a honeymoon?" he asked.

Her shoulder twitched again. "It's when the bride and groom take a special trip."

His eyes lit up. "To Disney World?"

"Yes, or the beach. It could be anywhere."

"I think we should go on a honeymoon!" he said.

"Yeah!" Nicholas chorused. "Let's go on a honeymoon."

Emily rolled her eyes in sisterly superiority. "We can't go on a honeymoon, you guys. Kids don't get to go. Just grown-ups."

Jeremy frowned. "That stinks."

"Exactly," Amy said. "We would miss you too much, so we're not going on a honeymoon."

Jeremy's face cleared. "Okay. Do we have any cookies?"

"Did you eat your peas?" Amy asked, glancing at the table.

Jeremy squirmed. "Two of 'em." He slid a glance toward Justin. "Do you eat peas?"

"Yes, I do. Peas make you tall."

Jeremy's eyes widened and he took in Justin's height. "They do?"

Nick smiled. "I'm gonna be tall," he said. "I eat 'em with catsup."

Amy turned away from the kids and whispered to Justin, "Peas make you tall?"

"Can't hurt," he said with a shrug, and nodded toward the kitchen table. "It worked."

Amy turned around to see Jeremy eating his peas. "Amazing," she muttered. "Teaching the twins the boy-way to pee, scaring away Ms. Hatcher, and now getting Jeremy to eat his vegetables." She glanced at him. "I'd almost have to recommend you for sainthood."

"Oh, no," Justin said, raking her from head to toe with another glance that turned up her body temperature. "I guarantee I'm no saint. I look forward to collecting the big one."

Amy tried very hard to prevent her mind from

venturing into forbidden territory at his mention of the big one, but she would just bet Justin had.... Her face heated. She definitely needed to chill out. "Ice cream," she said brightly. "Who wants ice cream?"

Later that evening, Amy collapsed on the sofa in the den and closed her eyes. She heard Justin's footsteps and felt his presence in the room, but kept her eyes closed. There was an air of expectancy between them. She ran her thumb over her wedding band, then lifted her hand in the air. "Why did you get me such a nice ring? You could have gotten me cubic zirconia."

A brief silence followed. "How do you know it's not cubic zirconia?"

Amy popped her eyes open and stared at him. "Is it?"

His lips lifted in a wry half-smile. "No, it's not. I've been called a tightwad, but even I know it wouldn't be appropriate in this case."

She pulled herself up into a sitting position. "In a way, it would be very appropriate," she said. "Our marriage isn't normal."

He raised his eyebrows. "From what I hear, normal isn't always that great. The ring is more a reflection of you. I think you're genuine, so I think you deserve a genuine stone."

Touched, Amy looked down at her ring, and the meaning of the band grew on her. It was one of nicest, sincerest things a man had said to her and it made her feel vulnerable and a bit confused. She slowly lifted her gaze to him again, too aware of her confusing feelings, too aware of the way his jeans fit his body and long legs like a lover's hand. Her fingers itched to trace the slight wave of his hair and the hard line of his chin. Her mind longed to know the secrets behind his eyes. Dangerous, she thought, and searched her mind for a safe subject. "How was your day at the market?"

"Profitable," he said. "My turn. What is a big one?"

Her stomach did a little dip. Not that again, she thought. "It's a relative term. Your idea of big and my idea of big could be very far apart."

"What about duration?" he asked, sitting beside her.

Amy's heart picked up at his nearness. "Again, relative. I would guess no longer than, say, three minutes," she said, betting that three minutes of anything with Justin couldn't get her into too much trouble. Three minutes wasn't long enough to— Well, if three minutes was long enough, it wouldn't be very good. Her cheeks began to feel hot again.

"Three minutes," he said.

She nodded, mesmerized by the intent look in his eyes.

"Of anything?"

"Within reason," she said.

"Okay, I want the big one tonight," Justin said.

Her heart stuttered. "So soon?"

"I told you I wasn't a saint."

She swallowed. "But if you use up the big one, you won't have it for later."

"That's okay. Three minutes," he said.

She swallowed again. "Three minutes of what?"

"One thing," he said. "A three-minute kiss."

Amy's breath stopped in her throat. "That's a long kiss."

"Depends on who you're kissing," he said and leaned closer.

Her heart hammering, Amy inched backward.

"Scared?"

Pride roared through her. She lifted her chin. "Of course not, it's just a kiss. Should I get a timer from the kitchen?"

He chuckled. "I have a timer on my watch. I can set it," he said, and pushed a few buttons on his watch.

Then he looked at her, lifted his hands to slide his fingers through her hair and pulled her to him like a bunch of flowers. As if the clock weren't ticking, as if he were in no rush, he rubbed his lips back and forth against hers, savoring the sensation of her mouth.

She sighed at his relaxed approach. He suckled her bottom lip into his, rimming just the inside with the tip of his tongue. Secret longings twisted inside her. Gently tilting her head, he stroked her scalp with his fingertips while his tongue toyed with hers.

Her breasts glanced his chest and his groan vibrated sensually inside her. Deepening the kiss, he trailed one hand down to massage her jaw.

A burning sensation built inside her. Inhaling his musky, male scent, she struggled with a restless need to take his mouth the way he was taking hers, to touch him, to get closer. She balled her fists to keep from reaching for him at the same time she opened her mouth farther for his exploration.

In a second, the tone of the kiss changed from lazy to hot and compelling. He tasted like sex. Consuming her lips, he slid his hand down her throat to her arm, urging her to touch him.

Her breasts felt swollen and her nerve endings buzzed with forbidden excitement. Her mind clouded with arousal, she leaned into him and lifted her hand to his shoulder. His strength lured her. Amy had told herself she always had to be the strong one, but his power surrounded him like a cloak, and the temptation to lean into him and absorb his power was overwhelming. Justin meshed his chest against hers, and the heat of him aroused her further. His fingertips grazed the side of her breasts, and Amy suckled his tongue deep into her mouth.

She burned. She wanted. He rubbed his thumb in a teasing movement on the outer edge of her breast. She wanted more. She wanted him to slide his hand under her shirt and cup her fully. She wanted him to rub her aching nipple, to take it into his mouth.

His finger edged closer and a moan vibrated in her throat. As if he could read her need, he moved slowly, ever closer to the stiff peak of her breast. So close.

Beyond the rush of arousal crashing in her bloodstream, she heard a tiny pinging sound. Justin paused and swore under his breath. The pinging grew louder. He pulled back, and she fought the instinct to follow his mouth with hers.

The alarm, Amy realized. The alarm had gone off. Three minutes had passed. Her body screaming for more, she disentangled herself and inhaled sharp breaths. The sound of her breaths mingled with his in the darkness like a hot sultry night, emphasizing the thick atmosphere of impending intimacy.

Rattled by the way he'd affected her in just *three minutes,* she stood and wrapped her arms around her waist. She knew without a doubt that the way he tempted her was more than sexual; it was also emotional. The knowledge frightened her so much her hands shook. She clasped either arm to halt the trembling.

Her mind whirled. She had always suspected Justin could be dangerous to her. His combination of strength, intelligence, and the underlying thread of his sexuality was entirely too compelling. She closed her eyes to calm down.

He touched her shoulder and she nearly jumped out of her skin. ''Don't!'' she whispered and held her breath. She was more sensitive than if she'd been sunburned. ''Please don't touch me.''

He didn't touch her, but his low murmur was almost worse. ''Okay,'' he said, so close to her ear, she could almost feel his lips again. A shiver ran through her. ''I want to do much more than touch you. I want to listen to your body instead of that damn alarm. I want to kiss you all over, but three minutes wouldn't be enough time. Three hours wouldn't be either,'' he said and the sensual promise of his words might as well have been an intimate caress in all her secret places.

''Sleep tight,'' he said, but it sounded more like a sexy taunt or challenge. Amy suspected she wouldn't be sleeping well tonight. She had grossly underestimated the effect he had on her.

An hour later, Justin rolled over for the twentieth time. He was still aroused. Although he'd sensed Amy was a passionate woman, he'd had no idea her response would burn his control to cinders so quickly.

Every time he closed his eyes, he tasted her lips and remembered the sensation of her tongue. He felt her breasts begging for his touch. He recalled the way her restlessness signaled her arousal. Every little move she'd made had wound his spring tighter

and tighter. It would have taken so little to go further, to push up her shirt and stare at her full breasts
before he tasted her nipples with his tongue. It
would have taken so little for him to push aside her
shorts and feel the inviting moistness between her
thighs.

She was his wife.

But she might as well not be.

Giving in to insomnia, Justin pushed back the
covers, rose from his bed and flipped on his desk
lamp. Turning on his computer, he scrubbed his face
with his hand. If he couldn't sleep, he may as well
study stock charts.

The following morning, Amy felt vulnerable and
she was angry with herself for the vulnerability. She
shouldn't have gotten so worked up over a kiss. *But
what a kiss,* her honest, feminine and currently un-
helpful mind said. She banged her glass of orange
juice down, and it sloshed all over the counter.

"Oops," Nicholas said.

Jeremy giggled. "Oops."

Together, they chorused, "Oops."

Her frayed nerves stretched tighter when the twins
joyfully chorused, "Justin!"

They were always so happy to see him, she
thought, and made a face in the direction of the sink.
The problem was she often felt just as childishly
happy to see him as the children did.

"Good morning," Amy said in a muted voice, noticing that his eyes were a little more narrowed than usual, and his hair was slightly mussed. Maybe he hadn't slept any better than she had, she thought hopefully at the same time she was ashamed for having such dark thoughts. He looked pretty darn good for having had a rough night.

"Morning, boys," he said cheerily, then offered the same muted tone back at Amy with a nod, "Good morning."

"G'mornin', Justin," Emily said in her sweet, sleepy tone as she spooned cereal into her mouth.

Justin returned the greeting. Amy's heart softened and she stroked her niece's hair. "I'll ask the Colemans if you can borrow their piano again today. Okay, sweetie?"

Her mouth full, Emily smiled and nodded.

"Who are the Colemans?" Justin asked.

"A family down the street. They've been kind enough to let Emily use their piano. I think she's interested in taking lessons." Amy hadn't figured out how she would afford a piano or the lessons, but she supposed that was a challenge for another day.

Justin nodded thoughtfully. "I'm heading over to my other home office, and I'm meeting some friends tonight, so I won't be home until late. You guys, give it your best shot to have a good day." He paused and met her gaze. "You too, Amy," he said in a deeper, almost intimate tone that tugged at something deep inside her.

That night, for the sake of sanity, Justin revisited his bachelor roots. He met Dylan at O'Malley's for beer and a burger.

"Michael will be late," Dylan said as he joined Justin at a table perfectly positioned for watching the wide-screen television playing the Baltimore Orioles game.

"Problem?" Justin said.

Dylan made a face. "Yeah, he's getting a home-cooked meal instead of a burger. I wouldn't be surprised if Kate has another baby soon."

"So soon?"

"I think they want a big family," Dylan said, and the look on his face reminded Justin of time spent at the Granger Home for Boys.

"Remember when everybody wanted a big family?" Justin said, taking a drink of beer.

"A big nuclear family," Dylan said. "We wanted Dad and Mom and a bunch of brothers and a sister or two to attract the girls when we were teenagers."

"It may not be nuclear, but you technically have a big family," Justin pointed out. "You're part Remington, so you've got two half-brothers and a half-sister."

Dylan laughed shortly. "Half is the operative word. Nothing would make them happier than if I disappeared. Especially Grant. He's the oldest and I know he thinks I'm trying to take over the entire company.''

Justin quirked his mouth in a partial grin. For the most part, Dylan concealed his competitive nature with a well-honed, cool untroubled air. ''And you're not?''

Dylan gave him a sideways glance. ''Careful, someone might find out I give a damn after all. I don't want control of the entire company, just part of it,'' he said in a voice that reminded Justin of a shark.

''No wonder Grant doesn't sleep well at night.''

''Enough about me. How's married life? How are the perks?'' he asked with a sly grin.

''Amy and I haven't known each other very long, so we're not to the perks stage yet.'' He gave a sigh of frustration. ''Besides I'm married to a descendent of Joan of Arc, so she doesn't believe she has any human needs.''

Dylan winced. ''Sorry, bud. But you know even Joan of Arc burned in the end. How's the rest of it? Are you spending money like water?''

''Not yet,'' Justin said, the prospect of uncontrolled spending threatening a bout of indigestion. ''I bought something today for one of the kids and I'm setting up accounts for their college education.''

Dylan raised his eyebrows. ''This sounds like the real thing to me.''

"The kids are very real," Justin said with a shrug that belied his true feelings. "Kids take a lot of planning. I always knew that. I didn't know they could be fun, too."

"And Amy?"

Justin thought about how responsive she'd felt last night and wanted to growl. "Amy could be a lot of fun if she'd quit trying to save the world for fifteen minutes."

"Maybe you can get her to save you," Dylan said with a wicked grin.

Amy sat alone in the darkness of her den. The children were blessedly asleep and she was blessedly alone. Justin still hadn't arrived home. She should be welcoming these precious moments of solitude with open arms.

Instead her gaze wandered to the clock. She wondered where he was and with whom. It was none of her business, she told herself and rose to pace the area carpet. After all, it wasn't as if they were married in the truest sense of the word. If his idea of going out with friends included seeing a woman who would meet his needs, then that should be fine with her. In sexual terms, she had no claim on him.

So why did the very thought of Justin with another woman make her heart pound with fury? If Amy looked in a mirror right now, she feared a green monster would be staring back at her.

The force of her emotion for him made it even worse. She should not care, she fumed. "This is why I didn't want to get married," she muttered. "Caring for a man too much just gets in the way," she muttered to herself. "Feeling too much for a man muddles the mind and saps the energy."

She glanced at the clock again. Eleven-thirty. She missed their questions. Her day felt incomplete without them. She missed those few moments when she allowed herself to give in to her curiosity about him. And she was frustrated with herself for caring so much.

Taking a deep breath to calm herself, she left the den and climbed the stairs. This was why she needed to rein in her feelings at all times. Tonight was a perfect reminder. Amy must depend on herself and no one else. Always.

Seven

The following afternoon, Amy found herself in a bind. The preschool children for the after-school program would be arriving any moment and her sitter had called with an emergency. She needed Amy to pick up Emily, Nicholas and Jeremy. Amy's back-up sitter was out of town on vacation.

Although she would almost rather chew nails, she tried to get in touch with Justin, first at his house. To her surprise, she found him at her home instead.

"What's up?" he asked.

Just hearing the strength in his voice calmed her. "I have a problem. My sitter's had an emergency, and I'm here doing the after-school program, so I need someone to pick up the kids from the sitter."

A long pause followed, and she held her breath. Regret seeped in. "Forget it," she said. "You don't—"

"For Pete's sake, give me a minute," he said. "The market's still open and I've got two possible trades left. I'll place limit orders. Where does the sitter live?"

Amy quickly gave him the address and directions all the while thinking how much she hated asking for his help at the same time she was heaving a sigh of relief. "I really appreciate this," she said. "I owe you a—" She broke off before she said "a big one." The big one had gotten her in big trouble last time.

"We'll see," he said. "See ya."

No sexy tease on the *big one* from him either, she noticed with an odd sense of loss as she slowly hung up the phone. Perhaps he wasn't so interested in the big one with her now. That was good, she insisted to herself over a huge sinking feeling in her stomach. That was wonderful.

She kept telling herself the same thing during the after-school program and while she ordered burgers at the drive-thru. Ordering burgers, however, reminded her of her wedding ceremony. Brushing aside her sadness, she lugged the paper sacks of fast food to the front door and prayed her day wouldn't be topped off by the arrival of Ms. Hatcher. Opening the door, she reminded herself to limit her gratitude to Justin. She didn't need any more of that kind of trouble.

It only took a second for Amy to hear the tinkling of piano keys. For a half-moment, she wondered if it was a recording, but the sound wasn't at all professional sounding. She quickly marched through the foyer to the formal living room to find Emily, and her brothers standing on either side like bookends, playing a spinet piano.

Amy nearly dropped the burgers.

"Emily?" she asked. "Where did the piano come from?"

The boys looked up. "Justin!" they chorused.

Emily whipped around on the small bench with a huge smile on her face. "Justin got it for us!"

Justin poked his head around the corner with the phone attached to his ear. He looked at Amy and didn't speak or wave. He just looked at her from head to toe and back again, making her nerve endings dance on end.

Amy took a deep breath and looked at the piano. Beautifully polished and golden brown with white ivory keys, the instrument fit perfectly in the room without taking up too much space. She couldn't have made a better selection. How exactly was she supposed to limit her gratitude on this?

Nicholas sniffed loudly and rubbed his belly. "I smell burgers."

"You can't have any cuz you puked in Justin's car," Jeremy said.

Amy winced. Oops. Men could be particular about their cars. She was surprised Justin was still in the house. She searched Nicholas for outward signs of illness. "Are you sick, sweetie?"

He shook his head.

"He got into the sitter's cookie jar and ate too many cookies," Emily said.

Nick stuck out his bottom lip. "Justin won't let me have anything to eat cuz he said he doesn't want me to get sick again."

Surprised at Justin's wisdom, Amy felt the force of all three gazes on her as if they were waiting for her verdict. "Justin is right. We need to let your tummy settle down before anything else goes in it."

Nick eyed the sack of fast food. "But what about my burger?"

"We'll see. I'll call the three of you in a few minutes," she said and headed for the kitchen. She rounded the corner and plowed into Justin. Still talking on the phone, he wrapped his arm around her to stabilize her.

Amy caught a mouthwatering whiff of his aftershave, and remnants of the emotions she'd felt when he'd kissed her rushed through her. Tough to hold a grudge after the way he'd come through for her today.

"Okay. I'll check my system tomorrow morning

for the correction,'' he said, then turned off the phone. ''My online trading system listed a wrong trade on my account and I just caught it.''

His green gaze searched hers, and Amy struggled with a deep vulnerability that swept through places she kept hidden inside her. ''What made you get the piano?''

His lips twitched ever so slightly. ''Who said I got it?''

She smiled and shook her head. ''Well, it's not Christmas, so I know Santa didn't bring it down the chimney. I thought you told me you were a tight-wad.''

''I am,'' he said. ''This is different.''

''How is it different?''

He shrugged with discomfort and took the food sacks from her arms to the kitchen counter. ''Emily wanted to take piano lessons, so she needed a piano.''

''Needed?''

''In the scheme of things, this wasn't a big deal, so don't make it one,'' he said, narrowing his eyes restlessly.

''It was a big deal for her and for me,'' she added, taking a breath and lowering her guard a millimeter. ''Thank you.''

Nicholas and Jeremy burst into the room, popping the bubble of intimacy forming between her and Justin. ''We want burgers! We want burgers!'' they chanted.

"The natives are restless," he said. "Better feed 'em."

Throughout the evening, Amy would almost swear there was an air of anticipation between her and Justin. It grew thicker with each passing minute. At unexpected moments, his gaze would catch and hold hers. Her heart was also doing unexpected things like softening toward him. Amy's emotions swung from attraction and fascination to fear. By the time she put the children to bed, she felt like she was stuck on a carnival ride.

She went downstairs to the den, waiting and wondering which question he would ask her tonight. Which of her many questions about him would she get answered tonight? After waiting several moments, she leaned back on the sofa. Forty-five minutes later she awakened, but Justin was nowhere in sight.

Both disappointed and peeved, she returned upstairs and saw the light under his door. Burning with questions and curiosity, she lifted her hand to knock. She stopped just before her hand connected with the wood. It was better to keep a little distance, she told herself. She needed to rein in her fascination. He might be her husband, but it was in name only.

Justin avoided Amy the following morning. Her eyes might be saying *yes,* but he knew what her mouth would say. *No.* And if he weren't careful, the idea of changing her no to a yes could become an obsession. Could? he thought with a mocking chuckle. Who did he think he was fooling?

Hearing the blessed sound of footsteps departing the house and the door closing, he headed to the kitchen for a cup of coffee. Spying a bag lunch on the counter, he wrestled with his conscience, then grabbed it and darted out the front door.

Amy was buckling Jeremy into his car seat.

"You forgot something," he said, running to her side.

She glanced at him and the bag, then shook her head. "No, I didn't."

Confused, he looked at the bag. "Isn't this a lunch?"

"Yes," she said, sliding into the driver's seat of her Volkswagen.

"Who's it for?"

She met his gaze and her lips tilted in a smile so sexy it affected him the same way it would if she were dragging her mouth across his bare abdomen. "It's for you," she said and pulled her door closed. "Gotta go. Have a nice day."

Justin managed, barely, not to gape as she pulled out of the driveway and the kids waved at him. He glanced down at the bag lunch in amazement. Amy couldn't know that no one had ever prepared a bag lunch for him before.

He opened it and looked inside to examine the contents. Turkey and cheese sandwich on wheat, granola bar and banana. And a note. *No cookies until I know your favorite. Peanut butter or chocolate chip?*

That red-haired witch, Justin thought and felt an itchy, impatient sensation crawl over his nerve endings. He'd gone to bed hard and wanting every night since he'd said his marriage vows to Amy. Ever since "I do" had meant "I don't," he'd been burning in his bed. He hadn't known Joan of Arc could be such a tease.

Both. Thanks, J.

For the third time, Amy looked at Justin's bold scrawl answering her cookie question and couldn't help smiling. So, she had more than one cookie monster living in her house. She slid the note back into her pocket and stored the information in her brain.

The kitchen timer dinged and she pulled the second batch of cookies from the oven. The aroma of fresh-baked sweets filled the air.

"Is it your mission in life to torture me to death?" Justin asked from the doorway.

Amy turned around to look at him and stopped short. His hair attractively damp and mussed from his recent shower, he wore no shirt and a pair of cotton lounging trousers that tied at the top and rode low on his hips. The sight of his bare torso and abdomen short-circuited her breathing.

"Well, is it?" he asked, moving toward her.

Amy swallowed and shook her head. "No. How am I torturing you?"

"Too many ways to count," he muttered under his breath and nodded toward the cookies. "The smell is distracting."

"They're a thank-you gift."

"For who?"

"For you."

He blinked, then shrugged his impressive shoulders and reached for one of the cookies. "I'm not going to argue, but why?"

"Because you picked up the kids for me and I heard your car sustained damage."

"You're welcome," he said and took a bite of the still-hot cookie.

His chest was extremely distracting.

"What are you staring at?"

Embarrassment rushed through Amy, and she swung around to avoid him. "Nothing," she said in a high-pitched voice while she quickly removed the cookies with a spatula.

"I don't think so," he said, his hand squeezing her shoulder. Urging her back around to face him, he studied her face. "What's going on?"

"Nothing," she insisted in the same damn un-convincing high-pitched voice.

"I don't believe you," he said bluntly. "Answer my question."

Darn. "If this is truth or dare, I think I'll take the dare this time."

"It's not truth or dare," he said, moving closer. "It's just plain old truth."

Amy sighed and looked past his right shoulder. "It's your chest."

He glanced down. "What's wrong with it?"

"Nothing," she muttered, unhappy with him for forcing her to answer. "That's the problem."

He wrinkled his face in confusion. "I don't get it."

"You don't have to," she said, knowing her cheeks were as red as tomatoes.

He lifted a hand to her face. "You're blushing."

She rolled her eyes. "You're so observant."

Holding her jaw, he studied her for a long mo-ment. She saw the moment the light dawned. "There's nothing wrong with my chest and that's the problem," he echoed in surprise. "You like my chest."

She bit her lip. "I didn't really say—"

She broke off when he lifted her palm to his chest. His warm skin and the thud of his heart against her palm wholly distracted her.

"I can't believe Amy of Arc likes my chest."

"I'm not Amy of Arc," she protested, but there was no oomph in her words. He moved her hand in a sensual circle over his skin, over the pectoral muscles, then down the center to his belly.

Amy's mouth went dry. "You work out."

"A few times a week." He released her hand, but she couldn't quite find the will to remove it. Meeting her gaze, he lifted his hand to her hair, then circled the back of her nape and slowly drew her to him. He dipped his head and his mouth hovered a tantalizing breath from hers. "What do you want?"

She whispered the only word her lips would form. "More."

Justin's tongue drew a circle around her inner lips. Amy's temperature immediately rose ten degrees. He slid his fingers through her hair and drew her against him trapping her hand against his chest so that she felt his rapid heartbeat.

The sensual pleasure of touching his bare skin made her wish she could feel him against her naked breasts. He slid his thigh between hers and the thin cotton of his trousers both tantalized and frustrated her. There was no mistaking the hard bulge of his crotch rocking against her. Amy slipped her fingers to the back of his neck, urging him on. He drew out every carnal urge she'd never thought she possessed. In the eyes of the law, he was her husband. For Amy he was still forbidden territory, but she was finding him too tempting to resist.

She was consumed with his touch, his mouth, his attention. She wanted him to consume her. He guided her in a sweeping, sliding motion over his thigh that teased her, and turned her damp and swollen. She stroked his tongue with hers, unable to swallow a moan.

He slid his hand down over the outside of her breast to her waist, then lower to her bottom. He shifted slightly so his masculinity rubbed against her intimately as he guided her in an undulating provocative rhythm. Amy's mind grew hazy with desire.

"What do you want?" he asked against her lips, his breath coming as quickly as hers.

"More," she whispered again.

He dragged his other hand to the hem of her tank top and slowly slipped his fingers up her waist and each rib until he slid one finger just underneath her bra. "Do you want me to stop?"

"No," she said, and he unfastened the front clasp.

"You feel so good," he muttered "I want to taste you."

Amy shuddered at the dark desire in his voice.

He toyed with her nipples, drawing tiny moans from her throat. Suddenly, he lifted her onto the countertop and raised her shirt to reveal her swollen breasts. For a moment, he stared at them, then met her gaze with an expression of barely restrained passion. He lowered his mouth to her nipple and made love to it with his tongue. At the same time he slid his fingers inside her shorts, past her panties to where she ached for him.

"Oh, Amy," he said when he found her swollen. "So wet."

She couldn't recall ever wanting to be the sole source of a man's desire and satisfaction this much before. She couldn't recall feeling so utterly female, so powerful, yet vulnerable within the same moment.

This wasn't just her gratitude over Justin coming through for her. It wasn't her appreciation for the piano. This man called to her in a way no other ever had. She didn't completely understand it, and wrapped in the cloud of arousal, she couldn't begin to explain it even to herself, but she wanted him to know her. As a woman.

She arched her breast farther into his mouth, and Justin slipped his finger inside her. He gently nibbled on the hard tip of her breast, sending a shower of sensations through her.

Swearing, he drew back and scored her with his gaze. "I want to be in you. I want to feel you wet and tight all around me."

She shuddered at the provocative bluntness of his words.

"It's either the kitchen counter, your bed, or my bed," he told her. "You choose."

Her heart fluttered wildly. "Your—" She swallowed over her suddenly dry mouth.

"Good enough," he said and lifting her in his arms, he carried her into his bedroom. With excruciating slowness, he eased her down the front of his body. "Last chance. Are you sure about this?"

Absolutely not, she thought, but more than her body was urging her onward. Doubts, however, slithered and crawled through her mind like serpents. Teetering on the edge of the unknown, she took a deep breath. "What am I to you?"

He stared at her without answering for a long moment. "You're a witch," he said.

Amy's mouth fell open. "A wi—"

"You're the witch who makes me hard and keeps me from falling asleep every night," he said, and the insult felt more like praise.

"You're Amy of Arc determined to save the world."

Irritation trickled through her. "I'm not Amy of—"

"I'm a pretty selfish sonovabitch, so I admire you for it."

Surprised again, Amy swallowed the rest of her protest.

He lifted his hand to her jaw and shook his head. "You are, by some stroke of fate or insanity, my wife. I need to know you. In every way."

His words clicked deep inside her. She couldn't

imagine refusing him. Anticipation tinged with the metallic taste of fear filled her mouth. Theirs would be no easy coupling. He would touch her in ways she hadn't been touched, make her feel things she hadn't felt before. There were doors inside her she'd kept locked shut from everyone, and she wondered how she would keep those same doors locked from Justin.

She couldn't begin to answer all her unanswered questions. Except one. "If I'm a witch and I've been keeping you awake," she said, twining her arms around the back of his neck to bring his mouth closer to hers. "Then show me how to put you to sleep."

His eyes lit like twin flames. "This is gonna take a while."

Eight

He led her to the bed and pulled her down on his lap. Lifting her tank top over her head, he pushed her bra from her shoulders so her top was completely bare to him.

"Your breasts have driven me insane," he told her.

Amy glanced down at her chest, expecting to feel her usual detachment about her body. Instead she watched his hand cup her, making her nipple pout. He made her feel so sexy. "I don't usually think about them," she confessed.

"I have," he muttered and pulled her closer to worry her nipples with his tongue.

In the mirrored closet door, she caught sight of the provocative image of his dark head buried in her breast. The sight and sensation provided a double sensual whammy, surprising her with immediate force. That was the tip of *her breast* his mouth caressed.

She had never thought she was a particularly sexual woman. Was that woman in the mirror really her?

He lifted his head and looked at her. Suddenly self-conscious, she ducked her head. She felt caught.

"What is it?" he asked in a low, intimate voice.

"I've never watched—"

Realization crossed his face. He stood and stripped off his lounge pants in one smooth motion. Amy stared at him. His body was unrelentingly male. Tugging her to her feet, he took her mouth at the same time he unzipped her shorts and pushed them down over her hips along with her panties.

He brought her lower body against his, then tilted her head toward the mirror. "Now look."

Her mouth went dry at the soft, sensual image of her body entwined with his.

"Nothing to say?" he taunted, stroking her breast with his hand.

She closed her eyes, but the strong, knee-weakening visual burned in her brain. "You are such a show-off," she said, biting her lip.

"What do you mean?" he asked, his sexy chuckle vibrating against her.

"I mean," she said, "your body is—" She stifled a groan of embarrassment. "Your body is impressive," she hissed through her lips.

"You're impressed with my body? I hadn't thought you'd noticed."

Hearing the smile in his voice, she shot him a dark look. "Liar."

His gaze grew serious. "Don't you know what a turn-on it is knowing such a sexy woman is impressed with me?"

"I'm not a sex—" she automatically started to say before he covered her mouth with his hand.

He shook his head in disbelief. "Teacher, somewhere along the way, your education has been sadly neglected." He rubbed his mouth over hers. "And I'm gonna show you how much."

He took her mouth and the room began to spin. Stroking her tongue with his, he tempted and teased her to respond. She'd thought it would be heat and fury, and maybe it still would be. She hadn't thought he would make her laugh and ache for him at the same time. How did he do that? she wondered.

"Look," he said. "Look at you." He shifted her in front of him. Burying his face in her shoulder, he skimmed his hand over her breast, down over her abdomen, then lower still between her legs.

Through half-closed eyes, she peeked at the erotic

sight of his large hands arousing her. But his touch was too distracting, her feelings too overwhelming, and her hunger for him too strong. She turned into him.

"Why won't you watch?"

"I'd rather watch you," she said, and he groaned.

Nudging her onto the bed, he followed her down, kissing her breasts, dragging his tongue over her skin. The tension inside her tightened with breath-taking speed. He dropped open-mouth kisses over her abdomen, whispering words of praise.

When he kissed her intimately, she stiffened.

"I want to taste you," he said, and his words melted her resistance.

His tongue sought her tender recesses while his hands stroked her inner thighs. He found her swollen bead of femininity and caressed her until she began to squirm. She felt hot and needy, full to the point of spilling over.

"Justin," she said, her voice husky to her own ears. She wove her fingers through his hair.

"So close," he said, flicking his tongue over her again and again.

Helpless against his sensual onslaught, she twisted beneath him. He devoured her and the coil of tension tightened excruciatingly. She arched, and a power surge ricocheted through her. She gasped in shocked pleasure.

Justin kissed his way up her body to take her

mouth again. The taste of her pleasure on his lips spun her around again. Before she could catch her breath, he pushed her thighs apart and holding her gaze, he thrust inside her.

Amy gasped. Despite her arousal, she felt overstretched. He was large and hard.

He made a sound that mixed pleasure with exquisite frustration. "Tight," he muttered and swore.

"It's been a while," she confessed.

"How long?"

She breathed and wiggled beneath him, feeling herself slowly begin to accommodate him. "A while."

He swore again at her movements. "How long?" he repeated.

"Do we have to discuss this now?" she asked, distracted by his sensual invasion. "Can't you think of something better to do?"

He looked at her as if she'd just completely shredded his patience. His gaze dark and primitive, he flexed his powerful thighs and pushed deeper inside her, stealing her breath again. He lifted her hands to the wooden posts on the headboard. "Hold on," he told her and began a mind-bending rhythm.

His chest brushed her breasts and he stole kisses with each thrust. She felt the friction of his legs against her thighs. With a long motion, he pulled his hardness nearly all the way out of her. Craving more of him, she arched and flexed around him in silent invitation.

He licked her lips. "You like the way I feel inside you, don't you?"

She felt him, tantalizingly out of reach, at her entrance. She wiggled.

He licked her lips again. "Answer me," he demanded.

Surrounded by him and her need for him, she felt as if she were at his mercy. It was humbling, liberating, and scary. Though she feared what she might be giving up, she closed her eyes and just for the moment surrendered to her humanness, to her need as a woman. "Yes," she whispered.

Covering her hands on the headboard with his, he took her with all the heat and fury his gaze had earlier promised. He stretched inside her, filling her so completely she felt as if every stroke of his masculinity provided the most exquisite, intimate massage.

She felt his tension rise with the force of a crashing earthquake. His body quaked and rippled as he took her to the top again. Amy fought her release, fought the dizzying oxygen-deprived moment of ecstasy. In a primitive feminine way, she wanted to experience every moment of his pleasure.

She felt it before she saw it. His body stiffened, then he closed his eyes. "Amy," he muttered in a sex-rough voice that called her to come with him.

His climax took her over the edge again, and her body joined his in a rocket to the sky, shooting like a star.

Moments passed before Amy could breathe normally. Her head was spinning, her ears ringing as if cannons had gone off. Distantly she felt Justin roll beside her, his chest pressed against her side.

Her heart pounded so hard she was sure he could hear it. She knew she had never given herself so thoroughly, and she couldn't remember feeling this vulnerable in her adult life. Ever. She wanted to be held. Badly.

"Are you okay?" he asked, and she closed her eyes to his inquiring gaze. If he couldn't see her eyes, then he couldn't read her turmoil.

She cleared her throat. "Yes."

"Sure?"

"Yes," she said too quickly. Why did she feel as if she'd splintered into a thousand pieces and all those pieces of Amy would never be arranged in quite the same way again? She suddenly felt the horrifying urge to weep. Gritting her teeth against the feeling, she stiffened her love-worn body.

Justin slid his arm around her waist and shifted her on her side so she was cocooned against him. He surrounded her and even though her mind was racing, some primitive part of her must have trusted him because her body relaxed.

"You blew me away," he murmured next to her ear, a secret that gave her a sliver of ease.

Although she suspected their "blowing away" scales were vastly different, the notion that she'd had a fraction of the impact on him that he'd made on her allowed her to breathe normally.

Several hours later, she awakened, disoriented. What was she doing here? This wasn't her bed. Justin's arm was still wrapped around her, serving as a reminder of their intimacy. Amy shifted slightly and her body reminded her more thoroughly with twinges from their lovemaking.

A silken thread of uneasiness twisted inside her. Something about this was too comfortable, she thought. It would be too easy to slide into a habit of counting on Justin. Even though they had connected in the most powerful, physical way last night, he hadn't spoken any words of love and neither had she. Her heart tightened.

She couldn't love Justin, she told herself. She didn't know him well enough to love him. Besides, if she gave her heart to him, then what would she have left after he left her?

Too disturbed to remain, she held her breath and slowly slid from his bed. Gathering her clothes, she bundled them against her and tiptoed to her room. She tugged on a nightshirt and panties and crawled into bed. She'd thought she would feel safer in her own bed, more like herself. But she still felt shaken up and bothered. Knowing tomorrow would require all the energy and clear-thinking she could muster, she told herself not to think about Justin. She mentally closed every door in her mind to him, and when he still crept in like a warm breeze, she pulled the sheet over her head.

Justin watched Amy from the kitchen doorway as she poured juice and cereal. He wondered why she had left. He remembered the intensity of their love-making, however, and combined with her inexperience, he'd guess she was knocked off-kilter.

She must have felt his gaze. She looked up from taking a sip of orange juice and choked. She rose quickly from the table and rushed to his side.

"I— You—" She cleared her throat. "Do you want some orange juice?"

"I can get it myself," he said, catching all the little signs of nervousness, stuttering, high-pitched voice, and fluttery eyelids. Deciding he might as well get it over with, he pulled her into the hallway for a moment of privacy. "You left," he said. "Why?"

She bit her lip. "I, uh…" Her eyes widened helplessly. "Too much," she said haltingly adding, "you."

"At first," he agreed, remembering how tight she'd felt. "But you got used to me."

Color bloomed in her cheeks. "I didn't mean that

way.'' She closed her eyes and shook her head as if this conversation was almost more than she could bear. ''I mean the whole thing was too much. I'm not used to making love like that.''

''I sure as hell hope not,'' Justin said.

Her eyes popped open. ''And I didn't think it all the way through, the ramifications to the children.''

Confused as the dickens, Justin put his hand on her shoulder. ''Amy, what are you talking about? Last night had nothing to do with the kids.''

Her gaze of distress slid away from his. ''Well, I didn't think about sleeping arrangements and how the children would feel about finding us in the same bed.''

''Wouldn't that be normal for a married couple?''

''If we were a normal married couple,'' she said. ''But we're not. And I started thinking about what we'll do when the two-year trial period is over and if you leave how much it will hurt the kids.''

But not her. Justin fought the stinging sensation he felt in his chest. He swallowed the bitter taste of regret. ''Sounds like morning-after remorse.''

''Some,'' she admitted.

''I can move out if that will make it easier,'' he said, thinking it would make life a damn sight easier for him.

Her eyes widened in fear. ''The children.''

He remembered and nodded at the bottom line. ''It's okay. I won't leave before the custody issues are resolved,'' he said, wondering if it would kill him. ''We'll just stay out of each other's way.''

She moved her head in an uncertain, helpless circle, but said nothing.

Justin wondered where he could find a pair of blinders so he wouldn't see her twenty times a day. And earplugs so he wouldn't hear her voice. And a clothespin for his nose so he wouldn't catch her scent at odd moments. He wondered how to wipe out the memory of how she'd felt in his arms and tasted in his mouth. He wondered how to erase the visual of burying himself inside her, feeling her let go and let him in.

He didn't know how he'd do it. He just knew he had to.

Amy left a bag lunch on the counter for Justin. When she returned that evening, she found it in the exact same spot she'd left it, uneaten. The cookies she'd made for him were also uneaten. When she caught a quick glance inside his room that evening, she spied a dozen stock charts posted on the wall. Remaining in his room, he didn't show up for dinner or afterward when she could have awkwardly attempted to explain her inexplicable behavior. Perhaps it was best that she hadn't had an opportunity to explain anything since she wasn't so sure she understood too much herself right now.

She only knew there wasn't much she wouldn't

do to give her sister's children a secure home and it felt as if Justin could threaten that goal at the same time he was helping to make it happen. He reminded her she was human, that she was a woman. With no effort at all, he made her aware of how much she could want. He added a dimension to her life that was thrilling and distracting.

The distracting part bothered her most. What she needed to accomplish was too important to get way-laid by a passion for a man with compelling green eyes and an inner core of power that drew her like a magnet.

So why was she thinking about him now? she asked herself as she prepared another bag lunch for him. She scowled, then wrapped two cookies in a plastic wrapper and put them in his bag. A vivid memory of Justin, his eyes lit with desire, his body naked as he thrust inside her, flashed across her mind. A rush of heat suffused Amy. Splashing her face with cool water from the water faucet, she de-cided she might have more in common with Joan of Arc than she'd thought. When it came to Justin, she felt like she was burning at the stake.

Finding the lunch untouched on the kitchen counter again the following afternoon, Amy reached the conclusion that Justin had put her on *ignore*. She couldn't, however, fault him for his treatment of the children. Emily drew some watercolor pictures for the walls of his bedroom as a thank-you for the piano. Amy noticed he praised the little girl for her effort. The boys swarmed around him for attention, and he took them outside to play a quick round of dodge ball.

She glanced at the lunch she'd left him and made a face. No surprise, but so far she was flunking Wife 101.

Justin acknowledged Amy with a quick nod as he headed for his room to bury himself in stock charts. Even in a wacky market, the stock charts made a helluva lot more sense than his witchy wife.

"Kate Hawkins called," Amy said.

Justin stopped. "What did she want?"

"To invite us to a barbecue. I accepted."

He nodded slowly.

"And the local stockbroker's association called asking whether you preferred beef tenderloin or seafood spinach crepes for the dinner where you'll be speaking. I told them beef. When the woman learned I was your wife, she invited me to come."

"You'd be bored," he told her.

She lifted her chin and met his gaze. "I told her to count me in."

Irritated and confused, he didn't bother hiding it. "Why?" he demanded.

"Careful," she said with a smile so sweet it made his teeth ache. "I might get the impression you don't want me to come with you."

"Like I got the impression you don't want to make love with me."

Her eyes widened in surprise and color rose in her face. She walked closer to him. "This is obviously difficult for you to understand, but nobody gave me an instruction manual for how to handle this situation. We don't have a normal relationship, whatever normal is. Believe me, I don't have one tenth your sexual experience, so if making love with you left me feeling totally unwrapped, it shouldn't come as a big surprise to anyone. Excuse me if I needed to catch my breath, catch my *mind!*" she nearly yelled.

Taken aback, he looked into her brown eyes flashing with misplaced indignation. He felt the slow drag of his gut, tugging him toward her again. It would be the death of him, he thought. "You never answered my question about your sexual experience."

"You're right. Unlike you, I could barely breathe let alone think," she fumed and turned on her heel.

He could just let her have her temper tantrum while he returned to his stock charts. In another life, he thought wryly and followed her into the den where she watched the children from the picture window. "How long had it been?"

She slid a sideways glance at him. "Three and a half years," she said in a low voice.

He blinked. "Why so long?"

She crossed her arms over her chest. "I was too busy. I worked while I was in college to help pay for my tuition. Relationships looked messy and I knew I didn't have the time or energy for them."

"Who was it?"

"A guy who was very persistent. He pursued me long enough to catch me at a moment when I was—" She shrugged.

"Weak," he supplied.

"Curious," she immediately corrected as if weak wasn't in her vocabulary.

"Did he satisfy your curiosity?"

She paused a moment. "Yes, but not much else."

Ouch. "Lousy lover?"

"I really didn't have any basis for comparison."

She surprised him again. "Your only lover?"

She nodded. "And last until you."

"You're telling me you've only had two sexual experiences in your life?" he asked, unable to believe it.

"No," she said. "After the first time with him, I gave it two more tries, then called it quits. Being with you was—" she said, taking a breath. "Very different. But you have such a huge—" she glanced at him "—ego, that I'm sure you've heard this kind of thing before."

Bowled over by her disclosure, he struggled with a weird assortment of emotions. He had an odd urge to punch the guy who'd taken her without taking care of her. On the other hand, Justin was fiercely glad he had been the man to show her the pleasure of lovemaking. He walked to her side and despite the fact that her back looked as stiff as a board, he curled his hand around the nape of her neck beneath her hair. Despite her *cajone*-breaking image, he suspected the woman needed gentleness, something he hadn't offered her so far. "I wouldn't have thought you were so inexperienced," he said.

She glanced up at him. "Why?"

"Well, hell, Amy, you're built like a woman who could pose for a man's fantasy magazine. You laugh and every male within earshot age four to ninety-four is vying for your attention."

"You really think I'm built like a woman who could pose for a men's magazine?"

Justin twitched at the thought. He rubbed his face. "Don't get any ideas. The local school board wouldn't approve and neither would I. I wish I'd known all this."

She took a deep breath. "That's what I've been saying. You don't know me. I don't know you. You don't love me," she said, searching his face. "But we're going to do this for at least two years, right?"

He nodded, wondering if two years would be long enough for him to learn everything about Amy he wanted to learn.

"If we had been dating for less than a month and

we made love, would you have necessarily expected me to stay the whole night?''

"After a night like that?'' he asked, and he watched her nod. ''I would have kept you in bed for three days straight.''

Her eyes widened. ''Oh.'' She gulped. ''I'm not familiar with the etiquette, so—''

He gently squeezed the back of her neck. ''Screw etiquette, Amy,'' he said as kindly as he could manage. ''This was about getting enough of you.''

Nine

Amy's stomach dipped and swirled at the expression on Justin's face. She was beginning to feel that every time she was around Justin, she was in over her head. She prayed that wasn't true.

How had they gotten into this discussion? she wondered desperately. How had they gone from a barbecue and stockbroker's dinner to the complete unabridged history of her dismal sex life? Eating glass would have been preferable to telling him about her lack of romance, but Amy had made a deal with herself. If she wanted Justin to answer her questions, and she grudgingly admitted she did, then she would have to attempt to answer his questions.

She cleared her throat. "Can we get back to the broker's dinner?"

"You'll be bored," he told her.

"No, I won't. It will give me a chance to understand more about what you do."

"I can show you charts anytime."

"It will be the first thing resembling a date that you and I have attempted," she said bluntly.

That stopped him. He looked at her curiously. "You want a date?" he asked, sounding surprised.

She stifled a sigh. "Yes."

He shook his head. "I wouldn't take anyone I liked to this meeting. Besides—" he said, breaking off as his gaze skimmed over her breasts and lower.

"Besides what?"

Clearly reluctant, he rubbed his mouth. "Besides, if I were taking you on a date, my mission would be to get you into bed."

His *mission*. At the thought of being Justin's singular sexual mission, Amy felt a shudder ripple through her.

"But not at a stockbrokers' meeting. In the past, I could have picked up a woman there, but—"

Anger shot through her. "Picked up a woman? Is that why you don't want me to go? I might be interrupting your happy hunting grounds."

"I said in the past," Justin told her.

All her doubts clamored to the surface. "Yes, and our marriage is a figure of speech for both of us, so what's to keep you from 'hunting'? For all I know you could be picking up women when you go out with your so-called friends.''

He looked at her with an incredulous expression. ''Are you jealous?''

Amy's fury increased tenfold. She sucked in a quick breath. ''I am not jealous,'' she insisted. ''But if you're going to seduce me, I might need to be concerned about safe sex.''

His eyes darkened and Amy quickly gleaned that she'd insulted him. ''I'm not the one sneaking away from your bed in the middle of the night,'' he told her. ''And if you were so concerned about safe sex, then why didn't you mention contraception the other night?''

Amy swallowed. ''I'm on the Pill.''

''Why?''

It was none of his business. ''Because my periods are irregular!'' she said through clenched teeth.

He paused a long moment. ''Okay,'' he said. ''You can come to the stockbrokers' dinner and meeting if you want.''

Too peeved to be reasonable, she barely resisted the urge to kick him. ''Never mind,'' she said with a sniff and went outside to play with the kids.

Justin felt the breeze from the door swinging in his face and thought about ripping it off its hinges. She was going to drive him insane, he thought. If his friends had been true friends, they would have locked him up and thrown away the key when he'd said he was getting married.

First she tortured him by not making love with him, then she blew him away by making love with him. Then she'd insulted the daylights out of him by sneaking away like a thief. When he tried to keep a sane distance, she insisted on attending a boring stockbrokers' meeting with him. She'd flattered him beyond measure when she'd told him she could neither breathe nor think after he'd made love to her, then she might as well have kneed him in the groin when she'd suggested he was *hunting*.

He swore under his breath. The only thing he'd been hunting for was his sanity. He glanced out the window watching her twirl Nick around in her arms. She was an angel and she was a mistress. She was exquisitely soft and unrelentingly tough. She was impossible to manage, and if he did what was best for him, he would get the hell out of her looney bin.

But heaven help him, now that he'd had her, he wanted her again.

Over the next few days, Amy was snooty to Justin in a friendly way if that were possible. She turned her nose up at him at night, but she always left a bag lunch for him. When he didn't eat it, the next day she left a Post-it Note on his monitor reminding him to eat lunch. That little Post-it Note gave him an odd, warm sensation. He tried to recall the last

time anyone had given a damn whether he ate or
not and he couldn't. That night they planned to join
the Hawkins's for a barbecue, and Justin found himself looking forward to the casual gathering. He
wryly wondered if his bride might unbend enough
to talk with him in the presence of other people.

"It's not nice to hold a grudge," Amy could hear
her mother say in her mind.

It may not be nice, but it's safe, she respectfully
replied. Much safer to hold a grudge and keep her
distance. It was difficult, however, to bear ill will
toward the man when he made Emily giggle with a
silly joke. He pulled into the long driveway of the
Hawkins's home and the children immediately
clamored to get out. Amy released Nick's car seat
belt while Justin took care of Jeremy's. Emily
climbed out with a large bag of chips in her hands.

"There you are," Kate Hawkins called, walking
toward them with her baby in her arms. "Michelle's
been waiting for you."

"May I push her in the swing?" Emily asked.

Kate smiled and smoothed Emily's bangs. "Of
course you can, angel."

The boys dashed forward. "Can we swing?"
Nick asked.

"It's all yours," Kate said, pointing to the swing
set. "Michael was determined to get the outdoor
gym up for the baby even though she's not ready

for it yet. I'm glad someone will enjoy it this summer." She glanced up at Amy and Justin and a wicked glint shimmered in her eyes. "Justin, you look remarkably at ease considering you're a family man, now. I expected twitches and shakes and ulcers."

Amy was the one experiencing twitches. "He's actually very good with the children."

"Wonders never cease," Kate said.

Justin gave a long-suffering sigh. "You're never going to forgive me for what I said at O'Malley's that night you overheard me, are you? Would it help any if I mentioned I've never seen Michael happier and you're the cause of it?"

Kate's face softened. She reached forward and gave him a hug. "Of course I forgive you. Something tells me you're facing your own challenges now." She glanced past them. "Oh, here comes Alisa. I'll be right back."

"I bet Dylan will turn cartwheels when he finds out Alisa's here," he muttered.

Amy watched Kate greet a slim woman with long straight blond hair. She glanced at Justin. "Dylan doesn't like Alisa?"

"They go way back," he said, carrying the food from the car.

"How far back?"

"Back to the Granger Home for Boys. Her mother was the cafeteria manager and Alisa used to steal cookies for some of us. She and Dylan developed a heavy-duty crush as teenagers. Dylan keeps asking her out, but she won't have anything to do with him." He cracked a half-grin. "As the stomach turns. About the stockbrokers' dinner," he began.

Amy lifted her chin. "Never mind."

"You're not gonna get snooty again, are you?"

She stopped midstep. "I'm never snooty."

He stopped and looked at her. "Yes, you are. You've been snooty since we talked about the dinner."

"I have not."

"Yes, you have," he said with maddening calm.

"I have not," she insisted.

He shrugged. "Then prove it."

She swallowed her trepidation. "How?"

"Kiss me," he dared her.

Her heart flipped over. She swallowed again. "Your hands are full," she said in a weak protest.

"My mouth is free."

She stifled a sound of *help*. She wasn't prepared to turn to brainless mush tonight, and she knew kissing Justin would affect her that way.

"Amy," Kate said, providing a ready distraction, "I'd like you to meet Alisa Jennings."

"Saved by the bell," Justin murmured.

Amy felt a rush of relief and turned toward Kate and the blond woman. "Gotta go," she said to Justin, quickly leaving his side.

"Amy, this is Alisa Jennings, and she met Justin when he was—" Kate broke off, waiting for Alisa to fill in the blank.

"Probably around ten," Alisa said, extending her hand to Amy. "I must congratulate you on getting a ring on Justin's finger. He's been antimarriage as long as I can remember, so you must be very special to make him change his ways."

Amy's stomach turned. Alisa obviously didn't know the circumstances surrounding her marriage to Justin. "Uh, I'm not sure I—"

"—well, you know what a good woman can do," Kate interrupted tongue-in-cheek and put a comforting hand on Amy's arm.

Alisa smiled. "Yes, I've watched what you've done with Michael."

Kate glanced at Amy. "See how smart she is? That's why I wanted you to meet her."

Amy couldn't help smiling at their female camaraderie.

"Plus she has all these stories about Michael and Justin when they were kids."

Her curiosity piqued, she met Alisa's friendly gaze. "Really? What do you remember about Justin?"

"He always worked, sometimes more than one job. He worked with the cleaning crew at Granger until he was old enough to get a better paying part-time job," Alisa said. "And he was the best money manager of any kid at the home. All the other boys would buy candy or sports equipment with their extra money." Alisa shook her head. "Not Justin. He saved it. Everybody was always trying to hit him up for a loan," she said with a grin. "But Justin set a limit of two bucks and he wouldn't lend any more until the previous loan was paid."

"Let's move toward the picnic tables," Kate said. "Did they call Justin a tightwad back then, too?"

Alisa's face softened. "No. One year, there was this kid who wanted to visit his family for Christmas, but they didn't have enough money for him to come home because his father was very sick. Justin paid for his bus ticket."

Kate stopped with a surprised look on her face. "Really? I would never have thought—"

Amy's chest grew tight at the image of Justin, as a child, sharing his very hard-earned money that way. Overwhelmed by a need to defend Justin, Amy had to interrupt. "I haven't seen this tightwad side of Justin," she blurted out, and bit her lip. "He describes himself that way, but I don't believe it. He bought a piano for Emily two days after I made an idle comment about her wanting to take lessons. And the after-school program I run has just received an anonymous donation."

Kate nodded in the direction of her husband. "Same thing happened with the home for unwed pregnant teenagers where I volunteer. When I asked

Michael about it, he was evasive. Sometimes I wonder if the three of them have been doing something together, but whenever I start to ask, he—'' She paused and smiled. ''He distracts me.''

Alisa cracked a grin. ''Isn't that one of the qualities of a good husband? The ability to distract?''

''Perhaps,'' Kate said. ''Have you found anyone distracting lately?''

Alisa's grin fell. ''Not really.''

''Kate,'' Michael called. ''Your mom's on the phone.''

''Oh, and there's Dylan. Excuse me,'' Kate said.

''I thought he wasn't coming,'' Alisa said under her breath after Kate left.

''Pardon?''

Alisa waved her hand in a dismissing gesture. ''Nothing. Dylan and I were close as kids, but we're not at all now.''

''Justin told me the two of you had a crush as teenagers,'' Amy said. ''He also said Dylan keeps trying to get your attention now, but you won't have anything to do with him.''

Alisa's mouth tilted in a sad, wry smile. ''Justin always had a knack for pinning the tail on the donkey. The way I look at it is history has already repeated itself where Dylan and I are concerned, and it doesn't need to repeat itself again. We met again in college and he—''

Amy could see Alisa's eyes deepen with pain and

even though she didn't know the woman, she felt the hurt echo inside her. "It didn't go well," she finished for her.

Alisa met her gaze and Amy had the sense that she'd just made a new friend. "Right," Alisa said and gave Amy a kind, but assessing glance. "I have a feeling Justin may have found exactly what he needs in you."

Amy looked across the yard at Justin, her *husband.* Her stomach dipped at all he was and wasn't to her. What if fate was involved between them in some strange, crazy way? What if this was about more than custody and the kids and Justin's deal with God? What if somebody somewhere had put them together because they were meant to be married?

The wayward thought danced lightly through her mind like a butterfly, but the implication hit her like a two-by-four. Fate? Meant to be? Those terms sounded awfully close to fairy tales, she thought, and she had given up on Cinderella before she hit twelve years old. Plus there was her history of non-romance.

But what if there really was a man in this world for her, and what if it was Justin?

Amy closed her eyes. Then heaven had better help them both.

The evening was a companionable time filled with children's chatter, lots of food, and threatening storm clouds. The sky finally burst open, and the group went scurrying toward the house.

Nicholas glanced back, pointing at the table in horror. "The cupcakes! I didn't get one!"

"I'll get them." Amy darted back to rescue the cupcakes, but Justin beat her and snatched the plastic container. Grabbing her hand, he tugged her out of the downpour to the closest dry spot next to the house.

Justin's hair was plastered to his head, raindrops dripped off his chin.

Amy shook her head and laughed. "You're so wet."

"And you think you're not?" He shook his head and sprayed her.

Amy lifted her hands to shield her face and laughed again. "Stop!"

She pushed her drenched hair away from her face and looked up to find his gaze lingering on her breasts. Glancing down, she saw that she was just as wet as he was. The rain had turned her T-shirt nearly transparent as it molded faithfully to her breasts. Embarrassed, she crossed her arms over her chest. "Oops."

His gaze met hers with a trace of something that looked very close to possessiveness. "Yeah. If there was a wet T-shirt contest, you would definitely win, but I don't want anyone else seeing you like that." He pulled his shirt over his head and transferred it to her.

It was such a chivalrous, protective gesture that she didn't know what to say. With the rain pouring down just two feet away, she stood there staring into Justin's eyes and a dozen feelings rose within her. Bare-chested because he'd just given her his own shirt, this was the same man who had survived the Granger Home for Boys and had given his money to a kid so he could visit his parents. This was the same man who always knew the bottom line, and this was the same man who had made love to her with a force stronger than the rain. Her husband.

Unable to stop herself, she stretched up on tiptoe and kissed him. She slid her arms around his neck and with her kiss, she tried to tell him things she wasn't able to articulate to herself let alone to him. She tasted his surprise and desire, and she felt the familiar insistent urge inside her for more.

He pulled back and studied her with hooded eyes. "What was that for?"

Speechless while her body hummed, and her mind and heart raced, she tried to make her brain work. "A thank-you," she improvised. "For giving me the shirt off your back."

He paused again, pushing her hair behind her ear. "Maybe you can return the favor sometime."

Later that night after the kids were tucked in, Justin found Amy downstairs looking out the window

at the full moon. "I wondered if you'd come tonight. You've been pretty busy with your stock
charts."

"It's getting near the end of the trading season,"
he told her, but he knew he'd been avoiding her. As
he looked at the way the moonlight glimmered on
her hair and he remembered the provocative image
of her nearly naked breasts, he wondered if he
should be avoiding her again tonight.

She looked at him curiously. "Trading season? I
thought the stock market was open year-round."

"It is, but there's a theory that the best time for
trading is between October and May. Since it's almost May, I keep a close watch on my short-term
positions."

"What do you like most about trading?" she
asked.

He enjoyed being the object of her feminine curiosity. "I like the illusion of control. I have no control over the market, but if I study stocks and apply
different theories to the charts, then I find my per-
centage of wins goes up."

"Do you celebrate when you win?"

He shook his head. "Not usually."

She studied him for a moment. "You don't usually celebrate when you win because you win all the
time."

"More often than not," he said.

She pushed away from the wall and pointed her finger at his chest. "If you're so good the stockbrokers want you to come talk to them, then 'more often than not' must be an understatement."

Capturing her hand in his, he lifted her impertinent finger to his mouth and gently nipped it, watching her eyes widen. "There's a fine line between confidence and overconfidence in trading. The difference can cost you a fortune. The reasons I've been successful are that I know the difference and I focus on the discipline and process of trading."

He darted his tongue out to taste and soothe her forefinger. As her gaze locked with his in sensual expectation, Justin wondered what it would take for a woman like Amy to fall for him. He wondered what life would be like to have a woman like Amy loving him. Dangerous thoughts. It was the kind of thing he'd never allowed himself to wish. He was pretty damn sure it wouldn't be wise to start wishing now.

She stepped closer so that her body barely brushed his every time she breathed. "You're like a book I never thought I wanted to read, but once I opened, it was hard to stop. Every time I learn something about you," she said in a low, husky voice tinged with frustration, "I want to know more."

She was so inviting she reminded him of a flower waiting to be plucked. In the corner of his mind, he remembered how she'd reacted the time they'd made love, but he allowed himself a kiss. Gently pushing her back against the wall, he lowered his mouth to hers, and she immediately responded by opening her lips and twining her tongue with his.

Her instantaneous, sensual response affected him like an intimate stroke. Aroused, he played with her mouth, tasting her and allowing her to taste him. With each stroke of her tongue over his, a visual formed in his mind of her kissing her way down his body. Her hair skimming over his bare skin, her hardened nipples taunting him with random touches in her movement down to his thighs. Even now, he could feel the tips of her on his chest.

His hands itching to touch her, he slid his hand under her T-shirt and cupped her breast. Her sexy sigh in his mouth was too irresistible an invitation and he slipped his other hand underneath her shirt so that he touched both breasts.

Amy moaned and undulated against him. Instinctively he pressed his arousal between her thighs and when she opened her legs, Justin began to sweat. He knew how she felt, how she tasted.

He felt one of her hands circle the back of his neck, urging his mouth against hers, as if she were hungry for him, as if she couldn't get enough.

The notion sent a firestorm throbbing through his blood. He rhythmically slid his tongue into her mouth and she suckled him in the same way her body would squeeze his hardness if he were taking her.

She moved restlessly against him and he felt her hand slide down to touch him intimately through the fabric of his shorts. He couldn't withhold a groan. He wanted her naked. He wanted her mouth on him. He wanted her.

"Touch me," he urged in a low voice against her sexy open mouth.

With unsteady hands, she unfastened his shorts and cupped his aching masculinity in her hand. The touch of her caresses made him feel as if he would burst. Looking into his gaze with eyes dark with desire, she rubbed the honey of his arousal with her thumb and lifted it to her tongue.

The sight was so erotic it nearly made him crazy. "I want to take you," he told her. "I don't care much where or how. I just want to take you now."

Everything about her was one big delicious, inviting *yes*. Justin slid his hands down to her hips. It would be so easy to push down her shorts and find her wetness. It would be easy to lift her and wrap her thighs around his hips. It would be so decadently easy to thrust inside her tight wet femininity.

His mind and body throbbing in anticipation, he took her mouth as he began to unfasten her shorts.

Distantly he heard a high-pitched sound outside the room. He was so intent on Amy that he let it slide. However, he heard it again. A child's broken sob.

Despite his raging arousal, the sound tugged at him. It cost him, but Justin pulled back to listen.

"Aunt Amy," Nicholas cried from the top of the stairs. "I had a bad dream."

Justin ducked his head and inhaled deeply. He could feel her body humming with the same need he had. He took another deep breath. "You need to go," he murmured.

Ten

An hour and half later after a chilly shower, Justin still burned for her. But he wouldn't go to her. Prowling his small room, he felt caged. As much as he wanted her, his *wife* was an incredibly complex creature. Bold and shy, she somehow also managed to be both fearless and vulnerable. Justin didn't want her running out on him again. When he made love to her again, he wanted her waking up beside him.

He wondered how their relationship might have progressed if they hadn't married for the reasons they did. He tried to picture dating Amy, but it was damn difficult with three kids, as good as they might be. He wondered again what it would be like for her to give her heart to him.

His chest grew tight at the thought. He'd never wanted a woman's heart before. Her body, her attention, maybe, but not her heart. That got messy. But hell, marriage was about as messy as a man could get. The problem with wanting Amy's heart was that he suspected if she gave her heart, she would want him to give his in return. Justin would almost rather give his wallet.

"Have fun," Amy called after Justin as he left for the stockbrokers' dinner. He looked almost as good in a tux as he did naked.

He made a face. "I'm speaking."

She shrugged. "Well, then break a leg."

"I'll try not to. Later," he said and the door closed behind him.

Amy immediately turned to the kids. "I'm going out tonight, so a sitter will give you pizza."

"Woo-hoo pizza!" Nicholas yelled.

Emily was more reserved. "Who's the sitter?"

"Jennifer Stallings. I think you've met her. She lives down the street and she's very nice and experienced."

Emily nodded hesitantly.

Concerned, Amy bent down and gazed at her niece. "What is it, sweetie? Do you feel sick?"

Emily shook her head. She hesitated again. "You won't get in an accident, will you?" she asked in a low voice.

Amy's heart twisted and she pulled Emily into her

arms. "I have every intention of not getting in an accident. I know it's hard not to feel scared, but we can't lock ourselves at home. Not you or me." She pulled back and gazed into her niece's pensive face. "I tell you what. I plan to be home by around midnight at the very latest, and when I get home, I'll pop in and give you a kiss. Okay?"

Emily relaxed slightly. "Okay. Where are you going?"

"To surprise Justin," Amy whispered.

Emily's eyes widened. "Is it his birthday?"

Amy chuckled. "No, but he's giving a speech, so I'm going to surprise him by showing up to listen to him. Could you keep an eye on your brothers while I get ready?"

Emily nodded, and Amy raced to her room and jerked open her closet door. Her clothing selection for a dinner party was dismally limited since during most of her life she dressed like an elementary school teacher. Fanning through her hangers, she finally chose a black sleeveless sweater-and-skirt combination. With heels and her trendy new faux pearl necklace, she should pass muster.

She didn't want to embarrass herself or Justin. Doubts niggled inside her. What if he wasn't pleased to see her in the audience? What if the reason he had discouraged her attendance was something other than boredom? Like a more experienced woman. Her stomach knotted at the thought.

Nerves rising to the surface, Amy dressed and applied make-up, smearing her eye shadow and reapplying. Horrified when a blob of mascara fell beneath her eye, she quickly blotted it, then approached her hair which balked at every effort she made to tame it.

"Why don't you put it up on top of your head like you did for the wedding?" Emily asked from the doorway.

Amy shook her head at herself and smiled at Emily. "Out of the mouth of my favorite girl. Perfect solution. What would I do without you?"

Emily beamed beneath her praise. "Do you want me to pick some flowers in the backyard?"

"Dandelions," Amy murmured picturing the backyard. Not weeds. She spritzed her hair with water, then scooped it up off her neck and began to pin it in place. "Thanks Em, but I have a few sparkly bobby pins I might use instead this time. Maybe you can help put them in?"

Emily did indeed help with the pins and Amy would have to say the five-year-old had far steadier hands than she did tonight. After giving the sitter instructions and kissing each child twice, Amy left.

The meeting was held at an exclusive club in downtown St. Albans. Amidst the luxury automobiles, she handed her car keys to the valet driver who looked at her car askance. Nerves and irritation bubbled inside her. "It's a classic," she said with a smile. "Make sure you take care of it."

She walked into the opulent lobby decorated with chandeliers, statues, and fountains and she located Justin's dinner party. Almost all the round tables of eight, including Justin's table, were filled. After a thorough search, she found one spot at a table near the center of the room and sat down.

Although she felt terribly out of place, she picked at her food and tried to remain invisible as the dinner conversation swirled around her. Stealing glances at the head table, she saw that Justin was seated between two beautiful, perfectly polished women who probably had not needed the assistance of a five-year-old to fix their hair. They were everything she wasn't, she thought and fought not to feel diminished. The brunette, Amy noticed, kept touching him. She fought a terrible tug of envy.

"It's packed tonight," the middle-aged man with the hideous tie beside her said. "Everyone wants to hear what St. Albans's premier stock stud, self-made millionaire has to say. I say he's been damn lucky and has just missed the speed bumps most of us hit."

Indignant on Justin's behalf even though the brunette was sitting entirely too close and he was smiling too frequently, Amy clamped back a hasty retort.

The young man on her other side shook his head. "I have to disagree. Haven't you heard? He's been trading for years. He didn't make his fortune overnight or with one big trade.''

''You sound like a Langdon groupie,'' Mr. Bad Tie said.

The young man shrugged. ''I'm intrigued, like about three hundred other people who are here tonight. If he can share his secret, I'll be more than happy to cash in on it.''

Mr. Bad Tie grunted. ''If it were that easy, everyone would be doing it,'' he said then turned to her. ''Allan Walters. I haven't seen you before. Which firm are you with?''

Taken off guard, Amy blinked before she shook the man's hand. ''I'm not with a brokerage. I teach—''

''—business or marketing,'' he finished incorrectly for her with a nod of approval. ''It's good for anyone teaching business to be exposed to this kind of thing, but I hope you tell your students this is rare and people can lose the money as fast as they make it.''

''Needs to retire,'' the young man beside her murmured for her ears only.

''I hear Langdon goes through women like penny stocks,'' Allan said with a sigh as he eyed Amy's cleavage. ''One of the luxuries of being young and wealthy.''

Insulted, Amy bit her tongue, then counted to ten.

"You seem to know a lot about Mr. Langdon. Have you met him?"

"No, but word gets around if you know what I mean."

"So, most of the basis for your opinion is rumor," Amy clarified.

Allan with the bad tie adjusted his tie. "Well, it's clear he plays the field. Look. He's got a woman on either side of him tonight."

"The only thing that's clear is that the seating for his table is arranged male, female, male, female," she said and tried to tell herself she was totally correct even though a part of her worried.

"Well, I know the guy isn't married because it would have been in the newspaper."

"I can't tell you much about Mr. Langdon's past romantic life, but I'm pretty sure he doesn't get his stock tips from the newspaper or rumor mill. Perhaps that's part of the reason he's so successful."

"Well said," the young man on her other side murmured to her. He extended his hand. "Ben Haynes," he said. "And you are?"

"Amy Monroe," she said, wondering if she would ever consider taking Justin's last name.

"You're not the usual type of woman who shows up for these things," Ben said as if it were a compliment.

"And the usual type is?"

He grinned. "Think barracuda."

Amy's stomach twisted. So her competition, if she were interested in competing for Justin's attention, which she wasn't, she assured herself, was a cunning sea animal that gnashed its prey to bits with sharp teeth. Her head started to throb. Maybe this hadn't been such a great idea after all.

At the head dinner table, Justin stifled a sigh. Despite the fact that he'd flashed his wedding ring and mentioned his *wife* several times throughout the meal, the brunette woman beside him, Gabi, whose name fit her perfectly, had hit on him so much he would need to check for bruises.

Justin wasn't chomping at the bit to step in front of this crowd. Although he knew many admired and respected him, just as many resented his success. They were professionals. He wasn't, therefore he wasn't supposed to be successful.

"Oh, Justin," Gabi continued, but he turned off his listening ear as he took a drink of water and the association's president climbed the small stairway to the platform.

"Ladies and gentlemen," the man began. "It is my privilege to introduce our guest speaker for the Spring meeting of the Virginia Stockbrokers' Association. This man started out on a shoestring budget trading low-dollar stocks, eventually building to high-dollar profits. His net worth is now well into the multiple six figures...."

Justin stifled a yawn and surreptitiously glanced at his watch. Another moment passed and the president finally said, "Ladies and gentlemen, I now present Justin Langdon." The applause seemed to fill every corner of the huge room, surprising the dickens out of Justin. He stood and climbed the stairs to the stage to stand behind the podium. The room was packed and the lighting so dark he couldn't make out many faces.

As if he were attending a twelve-step recovery meeting, he said, "Hello, my name is Justin Langdon, and I'm a—" he paused for effect "—tightwad."

In the audience, Amy's heart swelled with pride and something that felt very close to love. Justin was such an incredible man.

The crowd laughed, and Justin continued with his speech. "I know it must irritate the dickens out of most of you to know that I built my fortune off the stock market without the assistance of a stockbroker. More importantly, no stockbroker benefited with commission. But all I've done is become my own expert. My system of trading is designed specifically with me in mind—my goals, my never-ending study of the market, knowing how much I can risk and still sleep at night, and my commitment to trade with a minimum of emotion. You have to figure this out for each of your clients, and unfortunately, your clients aren't clones."

With the exception of the tightwad remark, everything he said resonated with his actions. From the beginning, Amy had sensed he was a man who knew himself well. He had been tested and tried and had grown stronger because of it. Amy sensed many people admired him for the money he'd made. She admired him for the man he'd become.

"Most of your clients aren't like me at all," Justin said, "so parts of my plan won't work for them. But I'm going to help you with a response for the next time one of your clients says something annoying like, 'I've read about how Justin Langdon turned his portfolio from three digits to seven digits all by himself. Maybe I should try that.'

"Here is the step-by-step process for how to do what Justin has done. Number one, cheap housing. Live in a one-room efficiency in an area of town where your lullabye each and every night will be the sound of fights in the streets followed by police sirens.

"Two, eat cheap. Your regular menu should consist of cans of beans and packaged macaroni. You're allowed to splurge and go out to eat once a year. To McDonald's." The sound of the crowd's chuckles rose to the podium. They thought he was joking, Justin thought, but he knew better. He had lived it.

"Three, no car for three years. Walk or take the bus. Every penny you would have spent on payments, maintenance, gas and parking goes into your trading account.

"Four, say goodbye to your sleep. After you start making significant money on the market, get a job working the midnight shift so you can stare at your monitor all day, then work all night.

"Five, no social life for three years straight. Beer is a luxury, decent wine is a dream." Justin smiled to himself figuring he'd eliminated ninety percent of the people who wanted to "do what Justin Langdon had done."

"Six, no dating for three years straight. Dating costs money and if you want to do what Justin did, you have to put every penny into the market."

He took a drink of water and surveyed the crowd again. Light glimmered on red hair about halfway back. He paused, narrowing his eyes. *Amy?*

His heart hammered with an odd kick of joy and confusion. When had she arrived? Why hadn't she let him know she was here? She glanced from side to side, then met his gaze and smiled as if she knew he was looking at her.

He took another drink of water and noted she was dressed in a man-killer black number that faithfully followed every curve. It looked like the men on either side of her were noticing her curves, too.

He continued with his speech a bit more quickly than he'd intended. Justin wanted his questions answered. When the older guy beside Amy locked his gaze on her cleavage, Justin had to resist the urge to jump down from the stage and punch him. Justin took a slightly more civilized course, deviating from his prepared remarks.

"I'd like to take this opportunity to introduce you to my wife. She came in a little late." Justin watched her face turn the color of her hair and her eyes shoot daggers. "Amy, don't be shy. Wave to everyone."

She did reluctantly, but her expression told him there would be hell to pay. Wrapping up his talk, he nodded to acknowledge applause, shook hands with the president, then strode directly to Amy's table.

A young man beside her stood and offered his hand. "Mr. Langdon, I'm a longtime fan."

Justin shook his hand and nodded, then reached for Amy.

"I was trying to be invisible," she whispered through gritted teeth.

"Not dressed like that," he retorted in a low voice against her ear.

"Amy," the older man said with sickening familiarity that matched his lecherous smile, "now I know why you were defending him."

Justin did a double take. "You defended me?" he asked quietly.

Although it seemed impossible, Amy felt her face grow hotter. "He was—" Flustered, she broke off and shook her head. "Later."

"She's a sweet little thing," the man said with a wink. "Nice work."

Amy felt so patronized by the man's attitude she wanted to throw water in his face. She glanced at Justin and saw his jaw tighten.

Justin smiled like a shark. "If you know what's good for you," he said in a voice frighteningly gentle, "you'll pick your eyeballs up out of my wife's sweater, you old goat. Let's go," he said to Amy and tugged her toward the exit.

"Why didn't you tell me you were coming?"

Amy scrambled to keep up with his long stride. "I wanted to surprise you."

"You succeeded," he said, leading her across the marble floor. "Why didn't you come to my table?"

"It was full," she said, and couldn't resist adding, "You were already surrounded by women. Attentive women. Where are we going?" she asked when he punched the button for the elevator.

He tugged his tux tie loose. "Just as you were surrounded by attentive men," he said with an edge to his voice that surprised her. "The association gave me a parlor room for my use this evening."

"Parlor room?"

The brass elevator doors whooshed open and he pulled her inside. "This may come as a surprise to you, but some people are actually impressed by me, Amy. Some people think I'm hot stuff."

"I do, too," Amy said, feeling defensive. "I just

probably think so for different reasons than many of the people in that ballroom."

"And what would your reasons be?" he asked, his green gaze glinting with challenge.

The elevator doors opened, giving Amy a moment to gather her wits. A moment didn't feel nearly adequate, she thought as he guided her around a corner and whisked her into a room.

"You were saying?" Justin prompted.

Wondering at his mood, Amy laced her fingers together and wished she hadn't felt so off balance this evening. "I admire you for giving a boy at Granger money so he could travel home to see his family." She saw a flicker of surprise cross his face and continued, "I admire you for not wigging when Nicholas got sick in your car. I admire you for being able to deal with me."

He cocked his head to one side. "What do you mean about my being able to deal with you?"

Uneasy, Amy turned away and tried to focus on the beautifully furnished parlor. "Well, you married me and I'm not really wife material," she said. "In fact, you would be safe in calling me the nonwife."

He walked up behind her. "You're going to have to explain this. I've never heard of a nonwife."

"In my case, it's a woman who didn't want to get married and has never believed she possessed an aptitude for wifely things. Add in the fact that I'm uncomfortable that I'm very attracted to you and have feelings for you, and dealing with me should be the most crazy-making thing you've ever attempted.''

The silence that followed was so swollen with secret hopes and fears that Amy prayed the floor would swallow her to put her out of her misery.

''Why did you come tonight?''

''I told you,'' she said. ''Because I wanted to surprise you and—'' She broke off. Too much soul-baring.

She felt him toy with a strand of her hair that had fallen from her upsweep. ''And I wanted us to have a few minutes without the kids. A few minutes of just you and me.''

''Just you and me would have been okay, but you shouldn't have worn this,'' he said and lightly circled the back of her neck with his hand.

She stiffened. She'd felt out of place and he was confirming that fact. ''Why? It's not nice enough?'' she asked, turning around. ''What's wrong with it? I thought I did pretty good considering I'm usually dressed like an elementary school teacher.''

''Your outfit's nice. It fits you fine. Too damn fine. The problem is every man in the whole blazing room wanted to see you *without* your clothes,'' he said, hands on his narrow hips.

Amy blinked. ''Oh.'' She felt her defiance seep out of her like air out of a popped balloon. She noticed again how attractive he looked in a tux. Curious, she met his gaze. "Well, I have a question. If every man in the room wanted to see me without my clothes, does every man include you?"

Eleven

He slowly walked toward her until he stood just a smidgeon away as he looked down at her. So much closer, but still too far away, Amy thought. Her heart beat faster at the expression on his face.

"I didn't mention any exceptions, did I, Amy of Arc?" he asked in a voice that had the potential to undo her.

"Don't call me that," she said.

"I just want my turn." He lifted his hand to her face.

She took a tiny breath. Her tight chest would allow no more. "Your turn?"

"You've been so busy saving the world. My

turn,'' he said, lifting her hand to his shoulder. "Save me."

Her breath completely evaporated. *Save me.* It was such a ridiculous statement coming from him. He was so strong, so centered. If ever a man didn't need saving, it was Justin. "The closest I came to that was when I drove you to the hospital," she said in a voice husky to her own ears.

He shook his head. "Come closer," he said, and lowered his mouth to hers.

He took his time as if he knew she needed time and attention. She needed these moments to give without the rest of the world pressing in on them. She didn't worry that the children would burst in on them or the phone would ring or Ms. Hatcher would pay a surprise visit. It was simply Justin and her. Mouth to mouth, heart to heart.

Although she knew there was a part of her still unwilling to surrender to this marriage because self-reliance had been her salvation for too long, she also knew there was a power to her growing feelings for Justin, a power she'd never experienced before.

She couldn't find the words, or maybe she feared saying them. She had to show him. The searching, sensual open-mouth kiss went on and on, warming her, building the coil of anticipation inside her.

"Too fast," he muttered. "I always want you too fast." He rolled his tongue around the inner lips of her mouth in an erotic motion that made her weak.

"I want to go slow," he said. "I want to kiss all of you."

He pulled her sweater over her head and disposed of her bra. He lowered his mouth to her swollen, aroused breasts and took first one nipple, then the other into his mouth. She went liquid and restless beneath his mouth. He moved his hands up her skirt and beneath her panties to touch her secret moistness. He slid his finger inside her and she gasped.

Unable to remain passive any longer, Amy unfastened his tux shirt and tugged it loose. Eager to feel his skin, she shoved both the shirt and jacket from him. She slowly rubbed her cheeks and mouth over his hard, warm chest, savoring the touch and taste of him, the clean masculine scent of him. The strength she felt here, she knew, permeated the entire man. The knowledge of that strength turned her on even more.

Strength deserved boldness. Her heart pounding, she lowered her hands to his waist, undid his pants, and eased the zipper down over his bulging masculinity. His quick intake of breath was a provocative invitation to go further, to give more, to take more.

Her inhibitions lowering with each beat of her heart, Amy felt the rise of feminine sensual power. It was a new heady and addictive sensation. She skimmed her mouth down the front of his chest and felt one of his hands in her hair.

"What are you doing?" he asked in a voice roughened by need.

"Getting closer," she told him and slid down his body to her knees, pulling his pants and briefs down as she went. She rubbed her cheek against his full masculinity, then kissed him. Taking him into her mouth, she savored the taste of his arousal and the sound of his pleasure. He grew harder and fuller in her mouth.

He tangled his fingers in her hair and muttered an oath. She lifted her gaze to his green eyes full of black heat.

He shuddered. "You have no idea how erotic you look between my legs with your bare breasts, sweet face and mouth on me." He groaned and tugged her to her feet. "I need to be in you."

In a blur of motion, he pushed away her skirt and panties. There was no bed in the room, only a love seat. Sitting down on it, he lifted her over him. "Hold on to my shoulders," he told her, and eased her down over him.

She sucked in a quick breath. He was so huge and so hard that for a moment Amy wasn't certain she could take him. She closed her eyes and felt herself accommodate him.

"You are almost too big," she whispered.

He gave a rough chuckle. "We just need to do this a lot so you'll get used to me."

"I'm not sure I'll ever—" She broke off when he guided her hips upward and down again. Pleasure rippled through her. He did it again, and Amy had never felt so voluptuous in her life. She began her own rhythm, riding him.

He took her breast into his mouth and the sensation zinged all the way to her core. She felt herself clench around him and he began a litany of oaths and prayers. Shuddering, she rode him until she went over the edge in a ripple of endless ecstatic spasms.

Justin thrust inside her, his face clenching from a scalding release. Aftershocks rocked through both of them.

Her knees weak, she gingerly slid to his side and wrapped her arms around him. She had never felt so powerful in a wholly feminine way, and at the same time so defenseless.

He drew her against him. "It's gonna take a long time for me to get enough of you, Amy."

Amy sighed and closed her eyes. For this moment, she would allow herself to lean on him and rely on his strength. Wouldn't it be wonderful if she could always count on him being there for her? The prospect filled her with a joy so intense it shook her. What if this truly didn't have to end?

Justin helped put her back together, making her laugh with how limp her limbs were as he dressed her. "What happened to your bones?" he asked.

"You melted them," she said, thinking he had also melted her heart.

He skimmed his hands up her bare legs to her

thigh. "I like you like this. I think I'd like to keep you this way. How long did you arrange for the sitter to stay? A week?" he asked with a ridiculous mock-serious tone.

She laughed. "You're so funny. Around midnight, I turn into a pumpkin."

Glancing at the clock, he noted the late hour and groaned. "Someday I will have you for a whole night."

She shuddered with pleasure at his wickedly intent expression. "If no one is sick and we find the right sitter," she said with a smile. "And the stars are in perfect alignment."

"It will happen soon," he assured her and walked her out of the hotel to her car. He helped her into her Volkswagen and kissed her before she left, making Amy feel savored and precious in a way she couldn't remember feeling before.

On the drive home, though, other, darker realities slid into her mind. Some very important things hadn't changed. They'd agreed to try this for two years. They'd signed a prenuptial agreement that defined the terms of the end of their marriage. They'd agreed they didn't love each other.

The final thought cut like a knife.

Justin paid the sitter before Amy could open her purse. "That wasn't necessary. I could've covered it," she told him.

He waved aside her protest and studied her carefully. She seemed uneasy with him again, and he wondered why. He wouldn't have thought it possible, but the sensual, giving woman who had taken him to the moon just hours before seemed to have erected a nearly invisible wall during the drive home.

"You're quiet," he said.

"I'm tired and I promised Emily I'd give her a kiss when I got home."

He nodded. "Okay."

She bit her lip and met his gaze. "You were wonderful during the speech and after," she said. "Wonderful. Good night."

Justin felt his mood sink. "Cold feet again?"

She paused, looking conflicted, and he had his answer. He bit back an oath of frustration.

"I think it's more because of a reality check than cold feet," she finally said in that too-quiet voice.

"Tonight wasn't real enough for you?"

She drew in a quick breath. "Our marriage doesn't feel real to me."

"Maybe if we slept together—"

"—I don't think that's the solution," she said. "It's more than that. When we made our vows, I pretended I was giving an order at Burger Doodle so I wouldn't hyperventilate. We promised to give this two years. If it were real, we would have given it forever." Her eyes filled with doubt he wanted to banish. She looked down. "We don't love each other," she said in a voice edged with pain. "And the cherry on top of the sundae is the prenup agreement.''

Justin tensed. His attorney had warned him that it wasn't unusual for wives to ask for changes after the marriage. It wasn't unusual for women to use emotional or sexual blackmail to get more money. Amy wasn't that way, he told himself. He hoped she wasn't that way. ''What do you mean? Do you believe the agreement was unfair?''

She shook her head. ''No, but think about it. A prenup is a plan to divorce. It's an instruction booklet for how to end our marriage.''

''Are you saying that if we throw out the agreement then you'll be willing to sleep with me through the night?''

Amy paled. She looked as if he'd slapped her. ''No, I'm not saying that at all. You just don't get it. This is about much more than a stupid prenup agreement. Much more,'' she said and walked away from him.

After that, Justin felt a distance grow between them. Amy was polite and kind, but reserved. He felt he'd had something at his fingertips, something precious, and he'd lost it. They had been so close. He'd treasured her trust and generosity.

Now it was gone. Living in the same house with her was painful, much more painful than Justin had ever believed possible. He couldn't recall a time when he had felt this much pain. Not even when his mother had left him at Granger.

His frustration and dark desperation seemed to grow with each passing hour. One day he ran out to pick up some computer equipment. It took longer than he planned. When he returned, he saw a different, late-model car and pick-up truck in the driveway. Two men were unloading swings. Curious, Justin followed the path to the backyard.

Amy stood talking to the men while they put the finishing touches on a wooden swing set. Emily stood by Amy's side and the twins ran in circles. Nicholas looked up. "Justin, Justin! We're getting a swing set!" he hollered. "Right now! And I'm gonna be the first to swing on it."

"Nuh-uh," Jeremy said. "I am."

"Nuh-uh," Nicholas said. "I am."

"Nuh-uh," Jeremy said.

"Nuh-uh," Emily said. "Aunt Amy and I are gonna ride it first because we're being nice, and you're not."

Nicholas and Jeremy abruptly shut their mouths.

Amy glanced up and smiled at Justin. His heart stuttered. She looked at him with a light in her eyes as if their argument from last week was forgotten. He saw the moment she remembered. Her smile faded. "I bought a swing set."

"So I see," Justin said.

"These guys say they can have it up by the time we finish dinner."

"Woo-hoo!" Nicholas and Jeremy yelled.

"What's with the different car in the driveway?"

Amy smiled sheepishly. "Part impulse, part practicality. It's tough buckling those car seats in the Volkswageon. I stopped by an auto sales lot on the way home and voila, I have a new vehicle."

Justin felt a trickle of unease. "Why didn't you ask me? I could've helped you out with the swing set and car."

"No, the swing set's my treat. I've been planning this for weeks. And it was time to trade the Beetle." She laughed, mostly it seemed, at herself. "That's what payday is for, right?"

His gut tightened. "I guess."

"Besides, it'll all balance out with dinner tonight."

"What do you mean?"

"Cheap meal," she said. "Okay, you guys, let's go inside and eat and give these men a chance to get their work done. It might be dark, but we might all get a chance to swing a little tonight."

She led the kids inside and they rushed to wash up for dinner. A vague darkness hovered over him even during the kids' exuberance. He was concerned about Amy's purchases. He hadn't thought she was an impulsive buyer.

He watched her from the kitchen doorway as she chatted with Emily. "Time to eat," she said and laughed at the boys. "Are you going to be able to sit still enough to eat dinner?"

"How still do we have to sit?" Jeremy asked.

"Just a little bit still," Nicholas said.

"Good, cuz I feel like jumpin'."

"I feel like swingin'," Nicholas said.

"Me, too."

"Sit down," Amy said in a sing-song voice, and the boys scurried to their seats. "Sorry for the gourmet fare," she said to Justin, "but there are times when the only appropriate choice is beanee weenees."

Justin's stomach immediately rebelled. His brain screamed in protest. A flurry of images raced through his mind. His mother once bought him a shiny fire truck and herself a new dress and shoes. For dinner, they'd eaten beanee weenees. Another time at Christmas, his mother had bought herself a new refrigerator and television and for Justin she had bought video games. The electricity had been cut off due to lack of payment, and he remembered eating beanee weenees cooked in the fireplace. He had eaten beanee weenees himself when he'd been putting every penny into his trading account in an attempt to form the security he'd never experienced as a child.

It was just too much.

He went to Amy and spoke in a low voice for her ears only, "I'm going to my house. I'll let you know when I'll be back." He didn't wait for her response. He just walked out the door.

Hours later, Justin sat on the leather sofa in the

darkness of his home pre-Amy. The silence was initially soothing, but now it felt too quiet. He'd grown accustomed to the creaks and groans of Amy's older home and the sound of children's chatter and Amy's musical voice. He'd grown accustomed to limited solitude.

Glancing at the clock, he thought he might be helping to tuck in one of the twins or reading a book with Emily. And after the kids were put to bed, Justin never stopped feeling Amy's presence. She could be at the other end of the house or asleep when he was not, but he always felt her presence.

He wondered if she ever longed for him during the long hours between darkness and morning. He wondered if he would ever stop longing for her. He felt as if he could see the missing piece to the puzzle of his life, but he couldn't hold it, and it frustrated the hell out of him.

He'd returned to his house for solitude and peace, but the solitude was suffocating and there was no peace in sight.

Later that night, the phone woke him out of a restless sleep. Justin automatically answered it.

"Hi, this is Michael. I just heard from Dylan and I thought you might want to go see him. He's at the hospital."

Alarmed, Justin sat straight up in bed. "He's hurt?"

"No. Alisa Jennings was in some kind of accident. It's serious. She's unconscious in ICU and Dylan's determined to camp at the hospital until she wakes up.''

"How did Dylan know she was hurt?"

"Apparently her mother's out of the country on an extended trip, so they couldn't reach her. They found Dylan's business card in her purse, so they gave him a call. He doesn't sound good. I'll get over there soon, but you're closer to the West County Medical Center. I tried calling you at your bride's house first,'' Michael said and let the question hang between them.

"I needed some time to think,'' Justin said.

"Hmm. Okay. Don't take too much time,'' Michael advised as if he'd learned something along the way about waiting too long. "I'll see you at the hospital.''

Pulling on his clothes, he grabbed his car keys and left for the hospital. After getting two cups of coffee from a machine, he found Dylan in the ICU waiting room, staring unseeing through the glass door at the nurse's station. Dylan, the most outwardly carefree guy Justin had ever met, looked as if he were facing death itself.

"Hey," Justin said, offering him a cup of coffee. "What happened?"

Dylan accepted the coffee, but didn't drink it. "She was running after a neighbor's dog that got loose and a car hit her.''

"Oh, God," Justin said. A picture of Alisa as a child slid through his mind. "She was such a sweet kid, and she grew up to be a beautiful lady. This is a damn shame. What's the prognosis?''

"They won't tell me much," Dylan said. "Serious head injury, internal injuries. They don't know if she's gonna wake up at all," he said, his voice desolate.

"Did they let you see her?"

Dylan hesitated. "Yeah. I told them I was her fiancé."

Justin did a double take. He'd known Dylan had carried a torch for Alisa, but he hadn't known the man was this determined.

"It was the only way I could make them talk to me. Besides, her mother is on one of those trips to Europe and Russia where they move around every two or three days. Alisa may not want me right now," he said grimly, "but she damn well needs me."

"How long have you been in love with her?"

Dylan gave a wry humorless laugh. "Forever. She's what I wished for before I knew how to wish, but I screwed up big time when we got together in college. I was so full of myself. I didn't treat her well. I'm paying now. God, if she dies, I don't know what I'll do."

"But you haven't been together," Justin said.

"You don't understand," he said looking at Justin with stark eyes. "Just knowing she exists and is alive makes the world right for me."

Justin felt an echo of recognition inside him at Dylan's words. Knowing Amy existed made the world a better place for him. He wondered what he would do if something like this happened to Amy. Just the thought scared the living daylights out of him.

What if Amy died? What if she wasn't even on the earth? What if he lost even the possibility of being with her?

Justin's stomach churned with nausea.

"When you're in love," Dylan said, raking a hand through his sun-streaked hair, "there's only two places in the world—where she is and where she's not."

Justin sat with Dylan through the long night, but in his mind, he was going home to Amy. That was exactly what he did the following morning. On the way to her house, he called his attorney and instructed him to dissolve the prenup agreement. When his attorney argued against it, Justin would have none of it. "Either you cancel it, or I'll pay somebody else to cancel it."

Pulling into the driveway at dawn, he felt a sense of resolve that went deeper than his bones. He strode into the house and headed upstairs.

Amy's voice stopped him. "How is Alisa?" she asked quietly from behind him.

He slowly turned to face her and drank in the sight of her in a nightshirt. He shook his head. "She's still unconscious, still in ICU."

She crossed her arms as if to hug herself. "It's terrible. I couldn't sleep. I tried to call you after

Michael called me, but you must've already left for the hospital.''

"Yeah, Michael's with him now. I needed to see you.''

Amy nodded. Her nerves were shot. "You're right. I need to talk to you.''

Justin held up a hand. "I have something to tell you.''

Terrified he was totally giving up on their marriage, she shook her head and spoke in a rush. "No. I need to say I'm sorry. I know this has been impossible. I'm sorry I haven't been anything resembling a wife. I've just been so determined and so scared,'' she said, that admission costing her, "that I shouldn't rely on you. Justin, you're so strong. You're the strongest man I know, and I want to rely on you, but at the same time I'm afraid to do that. There has never been anyone I could rely on. Both my parents were alcoholics and I learned at a very early age to be self-reliant. I don't know how to be more balanced,'' she confessed, feeling her throat tighten with emotion. "But I'd like to learn with you.''

Justin walked closer and stared at her. "I called my attorney on the way from the hospital.''

Amy's stomach sank. He was already initiating a separation. She was too late.

"I told him to cancel the prenup. I want you to marry me, Amy,'' he said.

Her head reeled. Unable to assimilate his words,

she shook her head in confusion. "I don't understand. I thought you'd had enough of our marriage and wanted out."

"I've had enough of pretending this is temporary, because it's not temporary for me," he said, slamming her heart into overdrive with his revelation. "I can't explain it, and I know it sounds weird as hell, but I think you and I were meant for each other. You are the woman I would have wished for if I'd known you existed. You make the world make sense to me. I don't—" He broke off. "Why are you crying?" he asked in horror.

Overwhelmed, Amy felt tears slide down her cheeks. "I thought you were leaving for good."

He pulled her into his arms and held tight. "No, the beanee weenees pushed a button, but—"

"Excuse me?" she said. "Beanee weenees?"

"Long story," he said. "It's one of those bad memory foods."

She winced. "They're Jeremy's favorite."

"He can have my share."

Being in his arms filled Amy with such warmth and hope. "I don't understand what you were saying about the prenup."

"Cancelled," he said. "We don't need a prenup."

"You didn't have to do that," she said, knowing it had been important to his sense of security. More than anything Amy wanted Justin to feel all the security and love he'd missed as a child. She wanted to be the woman to give it.

"Yeah, I did," he said. "I want a lifetime with you. I want a commitment with you with every possible string attached. I don't want you to get away."

Her eyes filled with tears again. "I have been so afraid of loving you, but I do. I love the child you were, the man you are and I want the chance to love the man you'll become."

He lowered his mouth to hers and kissed her with such tenderness and love that she was humbled. How, she wondered, had she gotten so lucky?

"I used to think my mission was marrying you for the sake of the kids. Now, I know my mission is loving you for the sake of me."

One week later, Amy surprised Justin when she arrived home with Chinese food and champagne, but no children in tow.

"Where are the munchkins?" he asked, giving her a welcome kiss.

"They're at a sleepover at Kate and Michael's house," she said, unable to keep a smile from her face. "We passed inspection. The kids are really ours now."

"Hallelujah," he said. "We should celebrate."

"That's my plan."

"Oh, really," he said, his voice deepening in approval. "What kind of plan?"

"I think you should take off all your clothes and go to bed immediately."

He scooped her up into his arms and strode toward the room they'd shared as husband and wife for the last six nights. "I'm not arguing," he said. "What about the food?"

"Later," she said, and they made very good use of their time making love to each other. Justin never ceased to amaze her with how easily he read her body. With each passing day, he seemed to read her mind and heart.

Afterward, Amy slipped on a chemise and brought the boxes of Chinese food and champagne to the bedroom on a tray. They took turns feeding each other. "Did you hear about Alisa? Kate told me she woke up, but she can't remember anything."

Justin nodded. "Dylan called today. I think he's just relieved she's going to live. He said he's sticking to her like glue even though she'll probably spit in his eye when she gets her memory back."

"I feel lucky," she said.

He nodded. "I don't even want to remember what it was like before you were in my life."

Her heart filled to overflowing. "There's something I need to say to you," she told him and took his strong, gentle hands in hers. No Burger Doodle vows for her. Looking directly into the eyes of the man she adored more than anything, Amy made promises she knew she would keep. "I take you, Justin Langdon, to be my lawfully wedded husband, for richer, for poorer, in sickness and in health."

She leaned forward and kissed him with all the love in her heart. "Forever and ever and ever."

"I take you, Amy Monroe, to be my lawfully wedded wife. I will love and stand by you forever and ever," he said solemnly, then lowered his head to whisper in her ear. "Even if you serve beanee weenees."

Amy laughed at the same time a tear fell down her cheek. He had told her many secrets during the last week including the beanee weenee story. "Now that is love."

*   *   *   *   *

*Watch for Dylan Barrows to be
the next Millionaires' Club member
to find true love in*

THE MILLIONAIRE'S SECRET WISH

*The latest book in Leanne Banks's
exciting miniseries*
MILLION DOLLAR MEN.
On sale in June 2001 from Silhouette Desire.

SILHOUETTE® Desire®

Get ready to enter the exclusive, masculine world of the...

Silhouette Desire®'s powerful new miniseries features five wealthy Texas bachelors—all members of the state's most prestigious club—who set out on a mission to rescue a princess...and find true love!

TEXAS MILLIONAIRE—August 1999
by Dixie Browning (SD #1232)
CINDERELLA'S TYCOON—September 1999
by Caroline Cross (SD #1238)
BILLIONAIRE BRIDEGROOM—October 1999
by Peggy Moreland (SD #1244)
SECRET AGENT DAD—November 1999
by Metsy Hingle (SD #1250)
LONE STAR PRINCE—December 1999
by Cindy Gerard (SD #1256)

Available at your favorite retail outlet.

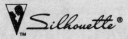

Silhouette®

January 2001
TALL, DARK & WESTERN
#1339 by Anne Marie Winston

February 2001
THE WAY TO A RANCHER'S HEART
#1345 by Peggy Moreland

March 2001
MILLIONAIRE HUSBAND
#1352 by Leanne Banks
Million-Dollar Men

April 2001
GABRIEL'S GIFT
#1357 by Cait London
Freedom Valley

May 2001
**THE TEMPTATION OF
RORY MONAHAN**
#1363 by Elizabeth Bevarly

June 2001
A LADY FOR LINCOLN CADE
#1369 by BJ James
Men of Belle Terre

MAN OF THE MONTH

For twenty years Silhouette has been giving
you the ultimate in romantic reads. Come join
the celebration as some of your favorite authors
help celebrate our anniversary with the most
sensual, emotional love stories ever!

Available at your favorite retail outlet.

Silhouette®
Where love comes alive™